GW00760827

VIOLET BLACK

EILEEN MERRIMAN

PENGUIN BOOKS

PENGUIN

UK | USA | Canada | Ireland | Australia
India | New Zealand | South Africa | China

Penguin is an imprint of the Penguin Random House group of companies, whose
addresses can be found at global.penguinrandomhouse.com.

Penguin
Random House
New Zealand

First published by Penguin Random House New Zealand, 2021

10 9 8 7 6 5 4 3 2 1

Text © Eileen Merriman, 2021

The moral right of the author has been asserted.

All rights reserved. Without limiting the rights under copyright reserved above, no part
of this publication may be reproduced, stored in or introduced into a retrieval system,
or transmitted, in any form or by any means (electronic, mechanical, photocopying,
recording or otherwise), without the prior written permission of both the copyright owner
and the above publisher of this book.

Design by Cat Taylor © Penguin Random House New Zealand
Front cover image by RuleByArt
Front cover background image adapted from iStock by Getty Images (1195447224)
Spine background image: iStock by Getty Images (1138384870)
Author photograph by Colleen Lenihan
Prepress by Image Centre Group
Printed and bound in Australia by Griffin Press, an Accredited ISO AS/NZS 14001
Environmental Management Systems Printer

A catalogue record for this book is available from the National Library of New Zealand.

ISBN 978-0-14-377542-3
eISBN 978-0-14-377543-0

penguin.co.nz

MIX
Paper from
responsible sources
FSC® C009448

Eileen Merriman's three young adult novels, *Pieces of You*, *Catch Me When You Fall* and *Invisibly Breathing*, were finalists in the New Zealand Book Awards for Children and Young Adults in 2018 and 2019, and all three are Storylines Notable Books. Her fourth young adult novel, *A Trio of Sophies*, was published in 2020 to huge critical praise and was also published in Germany. Her first adult novel, *Moonlight Sonata*, was released in July 2019 and longlisted for the Jann Medlicott Acorn Prize for Fiction 2020, with reviewers calling it 'skilfully crafted', and a 'carefully layered and thoughtful drama, with beautifully observed and believable Kiwi characters'. Eileen's second adult novel, *The Silence of Snow*, was published in September 2020.

Her other awards include runner-up in the 2018 *Sunday Star-Times* Short Story Award, third for three consecutive years in the same awards in 2014–2016, second in the 2015 Bath Flash Fiction Award, and first place in the 2015 Graeme Lay Short Story Competition. She works full-time as a consultant haematologist at North Shore Hospital in Auckland.

*To Lachie, who understands
the power and magic of the trilogy.*

CHARACTER LIST

SPIRAL FOUNDATION SURVEILLANCE FILE
CONFIDENTIALITY RATING: HIGH

BLACK FAMILY
Violet Black: survivor of M-fever; 17 years old
Nicholas Black: Violet's father; prominent research scientist
Ursula Black: Violet's mother; naturopath

WRIGHT FAMILY & ASSOCIATES
Ethan Wright: survivor of M-fever; 17 years old
June Wright: Ethan's mother; paediatric nurse
Freddie Wright: Ethan's brother; 5 years old
Lyndall Wright: Ethan's sister; 13 years old
Rawiri Sullivan: Ethan's best friend; 17 years old

OTHER SURVIVORS OF M-FEVER / VORTEX MEMBERS

Phoenix (Jonathan) Fletcher: 19 years old
Audrey Spelling: 18 years old
Harper Mehta: 16 years old
Callum Templeman: 15 years old

HOSPITAL STAFF

Zelda Glass: rehabilitation physician
Philippe Martin: physiotherapist

SPIRAL FOUNDATION STAFF

Noel Marlow: Director of the Spiral Foundation; neurologist
Melody Nenge: general physician
Greta Ziegler: neuropsychologist
Bruno Hoffman: junior doctor
Dash Petrakis: physical and weapons trainer
Jane Griffin: cardiologist

OTHER

Hans Bauer: Chief of Intelligence, International Terrorism Agency (ITA)
Thomas Neumann: microbiologist; anti-vaccination activist
Klara Becker: Thomas Neumann's wife; anti-vaccination activist
Dieter Fischer: engineer; anti-vaccination activist

ONE

VIOLET

The world is white and bright and terrifying. My head is an over-ripe watermelon, about to burst. My eyes are stinging, and my skin burns.

My limbs are heavy, as though someone has poured molten lead into my veins. I can't turn my head, can't speak, can't see beyond this white-white-white.

I'm dead, just like all the other kids this epidemic has taken away.

Hell is a bright light searing your retinae. Heaven is a myth.

I close my eyes. Wait for the reckoning.

TWO:

VIOLET

Violet. The name is a bubble inside my brain, perfectly rounded, but ready to burst as soon as I try to touch it. I've been here before, many times over recent hours-days-weeks. Stupid me, I can't stop reaching for that bubble, though.

Clinging onto life is a reflex, even when all else seems futile. My lungs are inflating, deflating. My heart beats a foreign rhythm.

Violet. Blink once if you can hear me.

How can I blink when I can barely open my eyes? But I do, so slowly I can almost hear my eyelids creaking. My virus-addled brain tries to make sense of the images before me. A pointy nose, black-framed glasses, a receding hairline. Who does this Picasso face belong to, and what is that beeping, and who is moaning? Not the Picasso face, not me . . . I don't think.

'Violet,' the voice repeats, and it's as if someone has raised a pair of binoculars to my eyes.

The world rushes in. It's almost too much. But I reach for that bubble, step back into the light.

Blink. Once, just once. The doctor smiles.

'Welcome back, Violet Black.'
He thought I was going to die, too.
I know that for a fact.

THREE:

ETHAN

Fact: Measles is a highly contagious disease that is easily spread by salivary or mucous droplets when coughing, sneezing or talking.

Fact: Measles can cause serious complications, from ear infections and pneumonia to the most life-threatening, encephalitis.

Fact: Encephalitis is swelling of the brain. It can kill you. Trust me, I know.

Fact: There is a highly effective vaccine for measles.

Fact: In the late 2010s, a fall in vaccination rates led to a measles epidemic. Many years later, a new, deadlier strain of measles began to circulate — M-fever.

Fact: There is no effective vaccine for M-fever. Yet.

Fact: Ten percent of all those infected with M-fever will develop encephalitis. Ninety-five percent of those with encephalitis will die.

Fact: Against the odds, I have survived. Don't ask me how, or why. I guess I was lucky.

FOUR:

VIOLET

i am a baby, even though I am seventeen years old. Learning to speak and feed myself and walk again, after four weeks with a tube down my throat to help me breathe, and other tubes going into my arteries and veins and bladder.

The day after I emerged from my coma, the sixteen-year-old girl in the bed next to me died. The doctors turned off her life support. I know because I heard the nurses talking around me, using words like *vegetative state* and *brain dead*.

I knew her brain was dead before I heard them say that. I reached out and there was nothing. No shimmer, no pushback.

The doctor who turned the ventilator off was thinking of his own daughter when he did that, the daughter who'd got away with a mild rash and a runny nose. He'd thought, *there but for the grace of God go I.*

I don't believe in God. Not anymore.

On the rehab ward, there are mostly old people recovering from broken hips or strokes, and generally falling apart in every way. Me, I'm being built up again, piece by piece. Seventeen years old and a survivor of the deadliest virus to infect children and teenagers since last century's polio epidemic.

Today I'm sitting opposite a woman with Smart-Glasses, which change colour on a daily basis. Today they're green. Zelda is holding up cards and I'm reading the words back to her. *Dog. Cat. Happy. Sun.*

'Wow,' Zelda says, after I manage to get through the whole lot without a single mistake. 'You're coming along pretty fast.'

I guess she's right, considering I could barely speak eight days ago.

'So,' she says, stacking the cards, 'can you tell me what day it is today?'

'Wednesday.' I don't have to think too hard about that one, not when it's in the forefront of her mind, ready for the plucking.

Is this recovery? Or is it something else?

'Good, and what date is it?' Zelda smiles. 'Don't worry if you get it wrong. I can hardly remember what the date is myself, most of the time.' I feel her make the connection, and of course it's the twentieth of September, because it's the anniversary of her father's death tomorrow. The memory is a strange colour, a mixture of purple and grey.

'The twentieth of September,' I say, backing off from the conflicting images swirling through my brain. I'm not sure which are Zelda's, and which are mine, and which could be . . . someone else's. It's freaking me out a bit.

'Great.' Zelda's thoughts are baby-blue again. I relax, at least until she gets me up to walk. My stick legs fold beneath me, a baby deer. Zelda hoists me off the floor, all fifty kilograms of me, and drapes my arms over the walking frame the physio gave me yesterday. I need to use it until I get the strength back in my legs.

'Don't worry, it'll come.'

'But when?' I'm shaking all over.

'Every day you will get stronger,' she promises. I don't know about that. I'm not sure if it's my muscles that are the problem. It's as if my brain has forgotten how to tell my arms and legs how they should move, and when.

When I sit down again, my t-shirt is damp with sweat. Zelda is already thinking ahead, planning the rest of her day, and that's when I see *him*.

No, not really. Not with my *eyes*.

'Is there someone else?' I ask. 'Like me?' That's not exactly what I want to say, but whole sentences are still difficult.

'Well, yes,' she says. 'There are . . . others.' But not many, I know. Most of those who were afflicted as badly as I was have died, just like the girl in the intensive care unit.

'No,' I say. 'I mean here. In this . . . place.' I sensed him this morning, when I was returning from my shower. Somewhere near, I think.

But I have no idea, really, how far my reach is.

I have no idea.

My doctor's forehead creases, then smooths out again.

'Oh, you mean on this ward? As a matter of fact, there is. Perhaps it would be good for you to meet each other.'

'I'd like that,' I say. I don't tell her we already met several days ago. She'd never understand.

I'm not sure I do either.

FIVE

ETHAN

Before I went into a coma, the world was mostly pretty orderly. Input = output. I guess you could say I was in homeostasis, a word our biology teacher uses a lot. He told us that homeostasis is the word to describe how elements prefer to be in equilibrium with each other, like if you put a glass of cold water outside on a hot day and it gradually warms up to air temperature. That's me. I like to be in equilibrium.

I am *so* not in equilibrium right now.

When did it first happen? I'm not sure. Maybe when I was waking up after nearly dying of M-fever, and I couldn't speak, but I was trying so hard to communicate and then . . . then . . .

I pushed. And something, *someone*, pushed back.

Her name is Violet. Violet, but she is sunshine-yellow, and I need to find her because I think she might be just like me.

SIX:

VIOLET

My mother comes to visit me this morning, Thursday. Dad has returned to work now he's figured out I'm not dying.

'Violet, you're so thin.' Mum prods my arm, as though I'm Hansel in a cage and she's the witch. 'What did you have for breakfast?'

I contemplate my toes. 'Rubbery toast. Soggy cornflakes.'

My mother frowns. 'Well, what would you like for lunch? I can go and get you something. How about sushi?'

'You could take her out for lunch,' says a voice from the door. It's Zelda. She's smiling, but her thoughts are exploding into my head so fast I can't keep up. I don't want to look at them, don't want to see her father hanging in the—

Zelda strides forwards. Her fingers are cool on the racing pulse at my wrist. 'Are you all right?' And just like that, the images dissolve, and it's me I'm seeing, my skin chalky.

'Just a bit of a headache,' I lie. In the doorway, a blur of movement. Looking up, I see a boy leaning on a walking frame. He's my age at least, with caramel hair and a long face, and he's thinking

Yellow

Violet, I think-say but I know what he means because he is

Apple-green

Zelda straightens up. 'Ethan, hi. Have you met Violet?'

Ethan shakes his head. It's confusing viewing myself through his eyes. I'm not sure I like what I see, this girl with stringy black hair and chicken-bone wrists.

'Nice to meet you,' Ethan says.

'Nice to meet you,' I reply, and in my head I feel a *click*, as if a pair of Lego blocks have slotted together.

Mum checks her watch. 'I've got to get to work, love, but shall I come and pick you up for lunch? There's a café across the road.'

'Actually, my head is quite sore.' I sink into my pillows. 'Maybe tomorrow.'

'No rush.' Zelda takes the tablet off the end of my bed, the one with all my notes and drug chart and observations on it. 'I'll get the nurse to give you some painkillers, OK?' Her fingers move over the screen.

'I think I just need to sleep.' I close my eyes, and in my mind, Ethan says *later*.

Later, I echo.

SEVEN:

ETHAN

i think maybe I died. Ethan Wright, dead at seventeen, never meant to come back. My brain is fried, a mass of melted wires, and now all these weird things are happening. Is this what it's like to have schizophrenia? I'm too scared to ask, especially after the dream I woke from this morning.

I'm seventeen years old, and I feel seventy.

Dementia, that's it. I must have dementia. Because if the dream is really true, then I — *we* — are in deep trouble.

I push my fork through my pasta. The menu said macaroni cheese, but I think they forgot the cheese. I'm contemplating messaging my mum to bring me something decent — a Mega Burger and fries, maybe — when I feel the air bending around me. Or perhaps not around me so much as inside me. When I look up, I see Violet pushing a frame, with her physiotherapist hovering behind her.

'Hi.' I nod towards the window. 'Parking's over there.'

For the first time, Violet smiles at me. 'Nice angle park.' She places her frame next to mine, and the physio helps her into her chair before leaving us there.

In the dining room, with all the other rehab patients. They're all about sixty years older than us.

Sneaking a peek at the hospital ID on her wrist, I note her birthday is in August, which means she is—

'Seventeen,' she says.

'Me too.'

'I know.' Violet's irises are espresso-dark, her forehead furrowed. 'When did you wake up?'

'Um, ten days ago, I think.' I set my fork down. 'Hey, don't.' She's rifling through my memories like she's in a record store or something. It's the weirdest feeling.

'Sorry, I can't . . . I don't know how to . . .' She presses her fingers to her temples.

'Yeah, I know,' I say.

'Before you got sick, could you . . . ?'

'No.'

'Me neither.'

Exhausted, we slump into our chairs. Ever so faintly, I hear Violet's heart skipping in her chest. This is so weird. I almost wish I could go back to how I was before, when I could only hear my own thoughts and heart and not every other damn person's bodily grossness.

Not that it's gross with Violet, but God, I hardly know her.

Violet exhales. 'How's the macaroni cheese?'

'It's pretty crap, but thanks for asking.'

She laughs, and just as abruptly stops. 'Do you get headaches?'

I nod.

'Do you get . . . memories?'

I glance around, then slowly shake my head at her. *Don't speak so loud.*

Violet looks, *is*, confused. *Why not?*

I've got a feeling.

What sort of feeling?

I think back to my dream and see her pupils widen, feel the squeeze of panic in her chest.

You made that up. That's a lie . . . isn't it?

I don't know. The dream-image of teenagers in pods won't go away. Perhaps it's from when I was in the intensive care unit. So why does it feel so wrong?

'It's an epidemic,' she says. 'Not an experiment.'

I lift my eyes to hers. 'Do you like coffee?'

'Sure.' She's shuffling through my mind again. I close her down.

'Sorry,' she says.

'S'OK.'

'Triple Jack,' she says. 'I like Triple Jacks.'

I grin. 'I love Triple Jacks.' Ice cream in coffee with grated chocolate on top — what's not to like?

Violet returns my smile, and as she does a memory flares at me, unrestrained. That's when I see *him* — oh crap.

Now things are really getting complicated.

EIGHT

VIOLET

My mother looks hurt. 'You want me to leave you there? So I'm not invited to this coffee date?'

'It's not a *date*. We just want to do something normal.' Admittedly, it may seem slightly odd that I want to go out for coffee with a guy I only just met on the rehab ward, especially when we're both still having trouble walking. 'Come on, I've been shut inside this hole for weeks. I only want an hour away from here.'

'I told you I was perfectly happy to take you out for lunch.'

'I know, and I'd like that. Another day.' I'm sensing I'm making too big a deal out of this coffee-date-not-a-date with Ethan.

OK, so it is a big deal, but I don't want everyone else to know that. I need to work out what this thing is that Ethan and I share.

'Fine.' Mum, distracted by chiming from her Personal Assistant, or PA, speaks into it, sending an Insta-reply. *New massage oil arrived yesterday. Have a look out back. Make sure you tell the customers about the two-for-one deal.*

'How's the new naturopath going?' I ask. Mum's last

workmate left suddenly just before I got sick, something to do with finding herself in Africa. Or maybe she was losing herself. How would I know?

'She's got a lot to learn, but I think she'll be good.' Mum takes the dropper bottle off my bedside cabinet and gives it a shake. 'I thought this would be running low by now. Are you using it?'

Keeping my expression blank, I say, 'I might have missed a couple of doses.' The tincture-of-whatever tastes really foul.

My mother purses her lips. 'I put this on your tongue every day when you were in intensive care. If only they'd let me give it to the girl next to you, then perhaps she'd have made it out of there too.'

'Mum.' I can hear her wondering whether she should take me to her rooms and give me a hot stone massage with healing oils, can hear her worrying about this date with a boy she hasn't even met.

'It's not a date,' I say.

Mum gives me an odd look. 'So you keep telling me.'

'Here,' I mumble, plucking the bottle out of her grasp, while making a concerted effort to shut out her stream of consciousness.

I'm not sure whether being able to read everyone's thoughts is all it's cracked up to be in sci-fi books and movies. I almost mentioned it to Zelda on the ward round this morning, but chickened out. What if she wants to keep me in hospital longer to run tests? What if they decide I'm crazy and transfer me to a psychiatric ward?

I've just subjected myself to a drop of Mum's foul tincture-of-whatever when I hear a bass voice rumbling in the hallway and purposeful footsteps. So much for blocking out other people's thoughts — I can hear my father coming a mile away.

Regression analysis raw data Violet must ask Doctor Glass is the work dinner seven or seven-thirty prototype must check half-hour not much time.

'Sweetheart.' My father is wearing his red suit today, complete with his favourite shiny black boots. I let him kiss me on the top of my head, and watch him kiss my mother next. Ugh, block-block-block, I don't want to know what they're thinking about when they kiss each other.

Or do I?

No, I really don't. It's like accidentally walking into your parents' bedroom when they think you're asleep. So gross.

'How are you feeling?' Dad asks.

'Much better.' I illustrate with a straight-leg raise. 'Zelda says I can probably come home next Wednesday.' Only five days away. I can't wait.

Mum drops her PA into her handbag. 'And she's going out for coffee with a boy she met down the hall this afternoon.'

'I see.' Dad's curious. He wants to know what this boy looks like, what his intentions are. *Ugh.* 'Does the boy have a name?'

'Ethan. We're bored. We thought it might be good to get some fresh air.'

My father sits on the end of the bed, adjusting his cufflinks. 'Of course, that's only natural. Tell me, why is he here?'

'He nearly died of M-fever,' I say. 'Same as me.'

'And recovered,' he says softly, and I'm confused by the eddy of emotions inside his brain, so viscous I can't make them out.

'Why are you dressed up?' I ask, although I have the answer before I've forced the question from my mouth.

Dad pinches his nose, glances out of the window. 'Press conference.'

'A press conference? Why?' Ever since my dad's M-fever vaccine failed, he's been avoiding the media.

He clears his throat. 'Well, naturally people are asking questions about my study. It's been implied that I used part of the research grant to fund my own activities.'

'Your own activities? Like what?'

His jaw tightens. 'People are accusing me of using a large portion of the money for our new house and car last year.'

My mouth falls open. 'That's a complete lie.'

'Of course. But that's what people are saying, and I intend to defend myself.' His emotions are streaming through to me unfiltered, a curious mixture of defensiveness-guilt-indignation.

'I think you should leave well enough alone,' my mother says, before muttering something about adding fuel to the fire. My father's face darkens, and I detect that they've already argued this morning. *If you just ignore them, the comments will die down, Nicholas. They're like schoolyard bullies.*

Are you kidding? You and I both know I never used any part of that research grant for my own gain.

Something else is coming through too, something far more disturbing.

It's a headline from this morning's e-bulletin.

M-fever deaths reach fifty in Auckland, with many more fighting for their lives.

Fifty? I thought my illness was a rare complication. I thought the girl who'd died next to me was one of the unfortunate few. What else are my parents hiding from me?

'I'd better get going,' Dad says, as I try to process that. 'I'll come back tonight, bring some pizza or something, huh?'

'Sure.' I don't want him to stay, nor my mother. All I can

think about is trying to read as much about this epidemic as I can before meeting Ethan this afternoon.

'Me too,' Mum says. 'So, two pm, was it?'

'Yes. Please.' I wait until I hear my parents' footsteps fade away before taking my own PA off my bedside cabinet. After calling up the internet, I ask it to search *M-fever deaths worldwide* and suck in a breath.

It's worse than I thought.

NINE:

ETHAN

Violet and I arrive in separate cars. Weird, considering we have the same departure point, but I'm pretty sure her mum wouldn't be able to help me out of the car, since I'm at least twenty centimetres taller than her.

I'm super-grateful to Philippe, the physio, for offering to help me from the Zuber to the café. Not quite sure how I'm going to manage my return journey, but I'll worry about that later. I could ask my mother, but then she might see Violet's mother. I'm not sure if Mum knows her, but she sure as hell knows who Violet's father is.

Nicholas Black is a dirty word in our house, the devil incarnate almost.

Scrap the *almost*.

I digress. Here I am, sitting by the window, the sun spilling over my hospital-white skin. In the Domain outside, the trees are bright with blossoms, pink and white. In the chair opposite me is Violet Black. For someone who's the daughter of the devil incarnate, she looks pretty damn good.

But this is strictly business. I can't let my attention wander like that, especially when she keeps randomly dipping into my thought-stream.

'Did you know about this?' Violet pushes her mini-Tab across the table.

I read the headline on the e-bulletin for the second time that day — *number of deaths from M-fever this year reach five hundred worldwide* — and nod.

'Apparently most cases are in isolated clusters,' she says. 'Mostly in New Zealand, Germany and Australia. This article says that ninety-five percent of all patients with encephalitis die.'

'Uh-huh.'

Once I've pressed send on our order, Violet says, 'So, we're in the lucky five percent?'

'Uh-huh.'

'Would you stop saying uh-huh?'

'I'm thinking.'

'I *know*.'

'Well, why have this conversation if you know what I'm going to say?' I glance at the counter, think about lowering my voice, and resort to the obvious instead. *Do you think the other survivors can do this too?*

I don't know. Violet takes a lump of brown sugar out of the bowl in front of us. *But when I try to . . . you know, reach out, I don't get anything back. Except from you.*

Sorry.

She averts her eyes, but not before I see a smile flicker across her lips. *You're not so bad.*

Maybe we're not close enough to the others to hear them, I think-say. *Like, I heard you before I left the ICU, but didn't hear you again until you were moved to the rehab ward. I guess you were too far away.*

Maybe. 'Thanks,' Violet says to the waitress, who has just deposited our Triple Jacks in front of us. *But you know what? Your thoughts are louder than everyone else's.*

Maybe because it's a two-way thing with us?

'Like walkie-talkies,' she says aloud.

'Like what?'

'They used to communicate with them in the old days. Two-way radios that people talked into. They got their name because at the time it was so amazing and new that you could walk while talking to someone who was miles away. Hard to imagine that being such a novelty.' She shakes her head. 'Don't worry.'

And I'm staring at her, while trying to pretend I'm not, and simultaneously blocking her — because I don't want her to know that I can't stop looking at the tiny freckles on her milky cheeks, and the divot that appears between her eyebrows when she's concentrating. Like now.

Why are you blocking me?

I frown. *I wasn't.*

Yes you were.

'OK, I've got a question for you.'

She looks at me. I look back at her.

'Your dad's Nicholas Black, right?'

'How do you know that?'

I tap my temple, point at her forehead. 'I saw him. The other day.'

She frowns. 'What else did you see?'

'Nothing. I wasn't *trying* to see it. You were having a really vivid memory.'

'Fine, yes, he's my dad. And?'

'Just asking.' I scoop cream off the top of my Triple Jack and suck it off the spoon. The cream-chocolate-cinnamon bursts into my mouth, so good that an 'mmm' escapes me. I don't think I've ever tasted anything this good. Has M-fever affected my taste buds too, or is it just that I've become used to the bland taste of hospital slop? 'He's the one who thought he'd made an M-fever vaccine, right?'

Violet's concentration-divot deepens. 'He *did* make an M-fever vaccine.'

'But it didn't work.'

She scowls at me. 'It isn't completely useless.'

'Did *you* get the vaccine?'

'Yes,' she snaps. 'And I'm sure you and your brother and sister did too. Did they get sick?'

'No . . .' I bite my lip. I don't want to argue with her, but from the expression on her face, I can see she's getting the gist of my thought-stream anyway. It's no different from what they've been saying in the media for the past few weeks. *M-fever researcher squanders two-million-dollar grant on flawed vaccine . . . or did he?*

'My dad didn't squander his grant,' she says. 'And if the government hadn't been in such a rush to release it to the general public, then he would have had more time to check his data and alter the vaccine so it had better uptake.'

'Sounds like you know a lot about it,' I say.

She rolls her eyes at me. 'It's not as if there's been any other topic of conversation in our house for the last few months. And I think I'll whack the next person who suggests my dad stole some of his research grant.'

'I never thought that.' Attempting to defuse the conversation,

I tilt my head to one side and give her a smile. 'But I'm a bit worried you're going to whack me anyway.'

Her lips twitch. 'Don't tempt me.' Her colour has changed from blue-green to icy pink, like the blossoms outside. I wonder if she can hear how my heart is beating double-time, the way I can hear hers.

Didn't mean to wind you up, I think-say.

You didn't wind me up.

I hesitate. *Hey. I meant to ask you. Have you been having dreams?*

What sort of dreams?

Like this, I think-say, showing her. *At least, I thought it was a dream, but now I'm not so sure. What if there's a room full of teenagers somewhere within the hospital, or in some research facility — teenagers like us, with tubes snaking in and out of their bodies and monitors above them lit up with images of their M-fever-damaged brains?*

Maybe they're the ones who never woke up, Violet think-says. *Maybe the doctors are trying to help them.*

But why haven't we heard about them? I slide the mini-Tab towards her. *Look it up.*

Look what up? Ethan's dream?

Yeah, you're funny. I lean towards her, as if to prove my point, because by now I know she's hearing my thoughts loud and clear. *What if they've found something that they think they can use? We'd be pretty useful for espionage, don't you think?*

I think you've got an overactive imagination.

Is that what you call this?

Violet scowls at me. *I think we should talk to Zelda.*

I think we should wait.

OK, then, we should talk to my dad.

No way.

My dad isn't the enemy.

I never said he was. Look, I didn't bring you here to argue.

Violet takes an aggressive slurp of her coffee. *You didn't bring me here, my mum did.*

Are you always this argumentative?

Are you always this controlling?

We glare at each other. Suck on our drinks.

I don't want our meeting to end like this. I don't want her to hate me.

'I don't hate you,' she says, her voice low. Behind her, the café door swings open, letting in a rush of cool air. Damn, it's her mother. Is our hour up already?

I'm glad you don't hate me, I think-say. *Because we've got lots more to talk about.*

Violet picks up a serviette and wipes her mouth. *Well, we can do that any time we want . . . right?*

And of course, she *is* right. At least while we're both in hospital, in close proximity, we can 'talk' to each other any time we like.

'Did you have a good time?' Violet's mother is wearing purple lipstick and a fake smile. She's wondering if I've been messing with her daughter. She has no idea.

'We'd have a better time if you'd let us have the whole hour, like I asked for.' Violet's surge of disappointment matches my own. I'm surprised, and delighted.

'Do you need a lift back?' Mrs Black clutches her micro-PA, which is one of the new credit-card-sized versions.

'No, thanks. I'll call my physio. Don't want you to end up underneath me or anything.' Oh no, did I just say that? 'I mean, if I fell over. You know.' *Ah man, kill me now.*

Violet's biting her lip. *I'm not laughing* at *you*, she thought-chortles.

Yeah, whatever.

'See you back in rehab,' she says, once her mother has helped her out of her chair.

'See you,' I mumble, my face still on fire.

TEN

VIOLET

C eleste, my best friend, comes to visit me today. She brings chocolate, nuts and gossip.

'Hector and Oscar broke up,' she tells me.

'Again?' Hector and Oscar are always breaking up.

Celeste cracks open a pistachio. 'Oscar says it's for good this time.'

'I give them a week. How about Mary-Ann and Nixon?'

'I don't know. I haven't seen much of them since school closed. But just after you got sick, Mrs Wu sent them out of English class because they couldn't keep their hands off each other.' Celeste strolls over to the window and peers into the courtyard. 'At least you got a single room.'

'Yeah, that's something.' Unlike Ethan, who is sharing with an elderly demented man who has an obsession with eighties music.

If I have to listen to 'Eyes Without A Face' one more time, Ethan told me last night, *I'll puke.*

We'd 'talked' for ages after the ward lights were dimmed. Not hard, considering lights-out is nine pm. I'd learned that Ethan has a brother and a sister, both younger than him. I'd learned that Ethan's mother is a nurse, and that his father had moved to the US when Ethan was twelve.

We hadn't talked any further about the dream that might not have been a dream. We didn't talk about the fact that we were freaks of nature. Instead, we'd discussed our own favourite music. Ethan had slipped his earbuds in while we were chatting and played me his favourite song. At the time, I hadn't even considered it weird that I could hear what he was listening to.

'. . . get to come home?'

'Hmm?' I focus on Celeste. 'Oh. Wednesday, hopefully. I might be able to get rid of that by then.' I point at the walking frame in the corner, which I'm starting to detest. 'How are the online classes going?'

Celeste purses her lips. 'No one's really doing any work. I spent all yesterday on ChinWag, can you believe it?'

'That sounds really boring.' The enforced quarantines over the past few months have led to a surge in social media use, even old ones like ChinWag.

'It's really boring.' Celeste breaks off a piece of chocolate before passing the block to me. 'I never thought I'd say this, but I'm looking forward to when they open the schools again. That's why I snuck out to see you.'

'Snuck out? Have you been grounded?'

Celeste hesitates. I can't resist; if she's not going to tell me, then I'll get the information I need anyway. Almost immediately, I regret dipping into her thoughts. A white lie would have been preferable right now.

'I'm not infectious anymore,' I say, feeling like Typhoid Maggie or whatever her name was, the woman who infected about fifty people with typhoid fever without even knowing she had it.

'I know that, but Mum's being mega-paranoid. Yesterday she wiped down all our groceries after they'd been delivered. We're not allowed to eat fruit unless it's been peeled, and she's boiling the hell out of all our vegetables.' She holds up a grape. 'If she knew I was eating these without peeling the skin off . . .'

'Well,' I say, 'she might have a point. I guess I could have caught it from something someone sneezed on at the supermarket.'

Celeste gives me a *whatever* look. 'You got it from Jasper, didn't you?' And the memory is so vivid, except it's her memory I'm seeing. There I am sitting on Jasper Sorensen's lap, and we're kissing like we don't have a care in the world. Did that really happen? And when? All the events from the week or so before I got sick are sketchy, as if parts of my memory were erased by the M-fever virus.

'So he had M-fever too?' Almost immediately, I wish I hadn't asked. *Oh. No.*

'He died,' she whispers.

I sink into my pillows and press my palms into my eyes. As if that will shield me from the images scudding through her mind: death notices and news items and funerals. *No, no, no.*

Ethan's voice drops into my head. *Are you OK?*

What's he doing, snooping through my thoughts?

I wasn't snooping, he think-says. *You were just being really . . . loud.*

Celeste clasps my shoulder. 'Violet, I'm sorry. I shouldn't have said anything.'

'It's OK.' I place my arms back at my sides. 'I didn't know him very well.' But I used to hang out with Tui Mitchell, too, whose name is also among the death notices I accessed from Celeste's memories. I need to get better at this blocking thing or I'm going to end up with post-traumatic stress or whatever it's called.

Celeste hugs me. 'I was meant to be cheering you up, not making you all depressed.'

'I had to find out sooner or later, right? I'm glad you came. Thanks for the food.'

'Any time.' Celeste scoops her bag off the floor, some blue faux-leather thing that matches her current hair colour. 'Better get home before Mum sends out a search party. Message me if you get bored, OK?'

'I will.'

Once she's left, I sit up and swing my legs over the side of the bed.

No, stay there, Ethan says. *I'll come to you. Unless you want to listen to Billy Idol, that is.*

I smile.

We sit side-by-side at the table in the courtyard outside my room. The table and bench seats have bird poo dotted all over them, and the sky is gunmetal grey. But there's a cherry tree in the corner with candy-pink blossoms, and for the first time in weeks, I feel as if I can take a deep breath. I smell damp soil. I smell the coming rain. I smell the warm scent of Ethan's skin.

It feels as though leaves are swirling in my chest, and I can't quite figure out why.

'You're lucky,' Ethan says. 'Having a room to yourself.'

I shrug. 'I guess it's because I'm a girl.'

He traces a circle in the dust on the table top. 'Come on, that's not why you got a room to yourself.'

'Are you suggesting I'm being treated differently from everyone else because of who my father is?'

'I'm not suggesting, I know.'

Fine. I think this conversation is over before it even started.

Ethan clasps my arm, stopping me from struggling to my feet. 'Sorry. I'm too blunt for my own good sometimes. Let's talk about something else.'

'Like?'

'I don't know,' he says — but I'm already thinking of my next question, one I don't dare speak aloud.

So, I can hear what you're thinking, and see and hear your memories, I think-say.

Yeah . . .

But I don't think I can smell what you can, or taste what you can.

Are you sure? Ethan plucks a leaf off the cherry tree and touches it with the tip of his tongue.

I frown. *It's probably good I can't taste what you can.*

Why?

Well, what if you have really bad breath?

Do I? He bends towards me, his dimples deepening.

No. And now I'm having to block him because I don't want him to sense the confused thoughts batting around my skull. He draws away and I feel him close me out, too. I'm relieved, kind of.

'I'm sorry about your friend,' he says.

My heart slows. 'Friend?'

'The one who died. Your boyfriend.'

'Jasper? You saw that?'

'Like I said,' he murmurs, 'you were pretty loud.'

I tilt my head back, taking in the sky. The rain-scent is stronger than ever.

'We were just having a bit of fun at a party. I don't know if anything would have come of it.'

Ethan inhales. 'One of my friends died too.'

'What was his name?'

'Her name,' he corrects. 'Selina.'

'Was she your girlfriend?' Am I jealous? No, why would I be?

'No. She was more like my sister. Our mums are good friends, so we'd known each other since we were little kids.'

'When did you find out?'

'Two days ago.' He lowers his head until it's resting on top of his arms. I'm not sure what to say, so I touch him, tentatively, on the shoulder. There's a tattoo on his bicep I've never noticed before, a snake curled around a rod.

'I got it last year.' His voice is muffled.

'Did it hurt?'

'A bit.' And now I guess we've answered my next question, because I can feel the table beneath my chest, can feel the needle darting in and out of my skin, and his heart . . . his heart . . .

'There you are,' someone says behind us. 'I thought you'd run away.'

We turn, almost as one. My father is standing in the doorway, weekend-casual in black leather trousers and a long-sleeved teal shirt.

'Ethan,' I say. 'Meet my dad.'

In the split second before Ethan shuts me out, I feel the golden swirl of his emotions turn grey.

I'm guessing my dad and Ethan aren't destined to be friends.

ELEVEN

ETHAN

On Monday, my physio says I'm doing so well that I can go home.

'What? Today?' We're standing in the corridor, my walking frame nowhere to be seen. My legs are still a bit wobbly, but they're holding me up.

Welcome back, Ethan Wright.

I blink. Was that my thought or someone else's?

Philippe crosses his meaty arms. 'Why not?'

Dismissing the random *welcome back* thought, I say, 'I'm not — I think I need a bit more preparation.'

'Thought you'd be dying to go home.' His expression doesn't change, but I can hear his internal wince. *Dying to go home, good one, Philippe.*

I'm not dying, though. Far from it. My body seems to be healing faster than I ever thought it would.

I wobble and resort to leaning against the wall. 'I am.'

'Steady on. We'll make it Wednesday, OK?' Philippe helps me to my room. I'm glad he can't read my mind the way I can read his, or he'd know I'm faking it.

I want to go home, I do. But not today. I need to prepare myself. I need to work out what to do about Violet.

Mum comes to visit me at two o'clock, before her shift starts on the paediatric ward. She's smiling, but I can sense her anger bubbling beneath the surface, as it has been for the past few months — ever since the first baby died of M-fever.

Those anti-vaxxers have a lot to answer for, she'd said. *And as for that Nicholas Black, they need to strip him of his doctor title and kick him out of the university.* She'd said he faked his data. She'd said he's been living the high life ever since he embezzled his two-million-dollar research grant, swanning around in his Mercedes Fuse SUV and talking to the media any chance he gets, while real doctors and nurses have been suffering from the longest wage freeze in years.

I'm not entirely sure what embezzling is, but my mum's a smart person. If she says the data was faked, then she's probably right. Still, a small part of me says, *What if?* What if Violet is right, and the vaccine just needed a few more tweaks to make it effective for everyone? And as for us survivors, what if this thing that's happened to our brains is part of some evolutionary process? Are Violet and I part of a new super-race? Is this why the Neanderthals died out, because *Homo sapiens* were more advanced?

Somehow I can't think of my mum as a Neanderthal, not when she's sitting there solving yet another Cubic Crossword. Even my new brain can't figure those out.

'What are Lyndall and Freddie up to?' I ask. As annoying as my kid sister and brother can be, I haven't seen them since last weekend and I'm starting to miss them.

'Freddie is at a friend's. Lyndall's at home, working on an essay. Speaking of which, it's about time we got you back into some study, don't you think?' Mum glances up, takes her glasses off.

'Study,' I echo. I used to think I wanted to do a marketing degree when I leave high school at the end of the year. My best mate, Rawiri, and I thought we'd set up our own company so I could market the virtual reality game we've spent years perfecting. But that seems meaningless now that people are dying around me. 'I don't know if I'm up to that yet.'

My mother gives me a sharp look. 'You need to exercise your brain too.'

'I am.' If only she knew. 'I'll be home soon enough. I can do it then.'

Mum brightens. 'Tomorrow, I hear.'

Seeing an electric-blue suit out of the periphery of my vision, I turn just in time to see a familiar figure whip past. *Crap.* From Mum's loud thoughts, I know it's too late to distract her.

She leaps up. 'Is that — how *dare* he show his face in here?'

'*Mum.*' I try to go after her, but my muscles can't keep up with my reflexes, and I end up sprawled on the floor next to my bed. Her voice echoes around the corridor. 'Have a word with you . . . Well, I know exactly who *you* are . . .'

Um, really sorry, I fire to Violet, before crawling to the doorway and struggling to my feet. Her father is standing at the end of the corridor, his arms crossed over his chest. My mum is standing about half a metre away, hands on hips.

'Have you come here to conduct more useless experiments? Well, I'll tell you what, once the government finds out how you really spent its money, you'll be smiling out of the other end of your digestive tract.'

Whoa, Violet think-speaks before emerging from her room, right next to where my mum is standing.

'I've come to visit my daughter, actually,' Nicholas Black says, ever-so-politely.

My mother glances between her nemesis and Violet. 'How ironic. I assume the vaccine you gave your daughter was just as useless as the rest of the batch.'

Black moves closer to Violet and slips an arm around her shoulders. 'She's alive, isn't she? Just like your son. If they hadn't received the vaccine then, God forbid, they may not have survived their illness at all.'

'That is complete—' my mother begins, but he cuts her off.

'I suggest you look at the post-marketing data before you let loose with comments like that. I refuse to be slandered by a rabid pack of so-called medical professionals. Hasn't anyone ever told you not to believe everything you read on ChinWag or whatever social media site you like to base your informed decisions on?'

I inch closer, my palm on the wall to steady myself. Mum's mouth has fallen open, as though she can't believe what she's hearing. A black fury thrums inside her. 'You're a liar,' she says, jabbing her finger at him. 'An unscrupulous, greedy liar.'

Worried Mum is going to hit him, I decide it's time to take evasive action.

As I slump to the floor and close my eyes, I hear Violet think-say, *You beat me to it.*

Wow, your mum really hates my dad.

Maybe not as a person.

You can't lie when we talk like this. You know that, right?

If you can then I haven't figured it out yet. I stretch, my fingertips contacting the wall behind me. It's almost midnight. Eighties Music Freak is fast asleep in the bed beside me. I'm not sure what's worse, his snoring or his music. *Sorry, once Mum gets worked up, there's no stopping her. I'm sure he's a good dad to you.*

He is, Violet think-says. I'm getting images of Nicholas Black hugging her and teaching her how to make pancakes. And yet I'm also streaming voice fragments, memories of *can't you see I'm busy right now,* along with images of an empty chair at a table set for three.

Well, I think-reply, *at least he's around some of the time.*

Do you know where your dad is?

I'm not sure. In Florida, last I heard. I keep hoping he's been eaten by an alligator.

Violet giggles, and I'm streaming yellow and thinking about how it would feel if I — no. No, I don't want her to see that.

Why are you blocking me?

I'm not blocking you. Perhaps my block isn't as impenetrable as I'd hoped, because Violet says, *I'm going to miss you too.*

Something flares inside me when she says that. Hope. Excitement. And something else I don't dare put a name to.

We can still meet up, I say. *Although maybe we won't be hanging out at each other's houses.*

Why not? Violet's colour has changed from sunshine-yellow to indignant purple.

Um, our parents hate each other? I mean, each other's ideas?

Oh, that's right, because I'm the daughter of an unscrupulous, greedy liar.

I don't think that. It's true. I don't know what to believe anymore.

Prove it, she says, before blocking me so fast I hardly know what happened.

Are you all right? I ask, after several snores from Eighties Music Freak.

Fine . . . Ethan?

Yeah?

Can you . . . ?

Sure. Someone might see me, one of the nurses, but what's the worst they can do? Send me to my room? I shuffle to the doorway and peer into the corridor. I can hear murmuring from the nurses' station, but I'm out of their field of view. They're drinking tea. I know that, because one of them is thinking about how much she's looking forward to a glass of wine when she gets home, and the other nurse is thinking about how she doesn't want to go home because she's sick of arguing with her husband.

I'm not sure I always like this newfound ability to read people's thoughts. It can be kind of disturbing.

Useful, though, because now I know they're completely distracted. It takes me less than a minute to reach Violet's room, less than a minute to creep behind the curtain around her bed.

Hey, I think-whisper. The only light in the room is that coming from the corridor. Violet's face is in shadow, but I can see that she's lying face-up, her hands tucked behind her head. I'm not sure where I should sit — the end of her bed? The chair?

Hey. Violet shuffles over and pats the section of mattress beside her. *Want to listen to some music?*

Sure. After lying down beside her, I take the earbud she presses into my palm and push it into my right ear. The music's not like anything I've heard before. There's a piano and drums, and, in between, a saxophone winding among the notes. Beside me, *inside* me, I feel Violet's heart thrumming blue.

'It's jazz,' she whispers.

'Jazz.' The word fizzes across my tongue. 'Does the song have a name?'

'"Blue Dream".' Her breath brushes my cheek.

I should have guessed. I've slipped into think-speak.

How?

Because it's a perfect description of you.

And I could block her out, I could, but now she's glowing blue-purple-pink, so I turn towards her, half-expecting a nurse to come crashing in, or her dad, or my mum, who knows.

But they don't. They don't, and when I kiss Violet Black, *this is going to blow your mind* takes on a whole new meaning.

My mind is wide open, a highway of impossibility. No, not *my* mind.

Our mind.

TWELVE:

VIOLET

When I wake on Monday morning, the blinds are rimmed with sunshine already. It's after eight. How did I sleep for so long?

I'm happy and depressed, all at once.

Ethan kissed me last night. Once, twice, three times before we heard footsteps in the corridor and he had to sneak back to his room. Kissing Ethan is like diving into a tropical ocean, warm and blue and limitless.

Whoa, he said after the first kiss. *Did you feel that?*

And of course, I *did* feel it — the way his pulse sped up to match mine, our inhalation and exhalation perfectly matched, our nerves humming in synchrony — as if we'd merged into one organism.

Kissing Jasper was nothing like that. I don't think kissing *anyone* else could be like that.

But I'm depressed too, because today Ethan is going home. Tonight I'll be alone for the first time since I felt Ethan's newly conscious mind nudging mine just over two weeks ago.

A voice slips into my head. *Morning.*

I roll onto my side and slide my covers over my head. *When are you leaving?*

Trying to get rid of me already?

No. I didn't know you could get awkward silences with this telepathy thing, but here we are. Awk-ward, especially when I catch a glimpse of what he's thinking before he closes me out.

Hey, I think-speak. Ethan's colour has morphed from cool green to hot pink. It's kind of cute.

X-rated, he think-says. *Sorry.*

I don't mind X-rated, I bluff. *When's your mum picking you up?*

In about an hour.

An hour? I think-reply, before worrying that maybe Ethan will think I'm being needy.

His laughter ripples through me, a sensation rather than a sound. *I don't think you're the needy type.*

Crap. How can he block me whenever he wants, but I'm so . . . open?

Don't worry about it, Vi. Can I come and say goodbye?

Goodbyes suck, especially when you're in hospital with people coming in and out every five minutes to take your blood pressure/deliver breakfast/ask if you want a bloody cup of tea.

I don't want a bloody cup of tea.

I don't want to say goodbye.

Ethan is sitting in the chair beside my bed, looking at least two years older in jeans and a Watermelon t-shirt, his hair sticking up in at least five different directions.

Watermelon is Ethan's favourite band. We listened to them for nearly an hour after he snuck back to his own room last night. No wonder I slept in.

'Is that how you wear your hair in the real world?' I ask.

Ethan shrugs. 'Yeah, but it's heaps longer than usual at the moment.' He's even got shoes on, red with black stripes down the side. 'I need a haircut.'

'Me too.' This conversation is depressingly normal. I shove my breakfast tray aside — I've had enough of cold toast and soggy cornflakes — and swivel to face him. 'Um. Do you think we'll be able to do this after you go home?'

'What, this?' He leans forward to kiss me, ever-so-briefly, on the lips. My whole body begins to tingle, inside and out.

'Not that. I mean, yes, that too.' I return the kiss — too bad if someone walks in — before switching to think-speak. *I mean this. What do you think our range might be?*

Ethan's forehead creases. *I have no idea. I think we're getting stronger though, don't you?*

I nod. Ethan hesitates, then touches a button on the remote beside my pillow, and the curtain slides around my bed, shielding us from the rest of the room. He sits beside me. *I need to tell you something.*

Fear jabs my chest. *What?* Is he going to dump me before we've even begun? Is there a girlfriend he hasn't told me about?

Block, block, block.

'Relax,' he whispers, his hand on my wrist. And when he kisses the side of my neck, I feel the blood surging beneath my skin, his and mine, and for a moment I forget where we are.

That is, until Ethan think-says, *I found someone else this morning. Someone like us.*

I barely have time to consider what that could mean — for him, for me, for *us*, when the curtain parts.

'*There* you are.' It's Ethan's mother. She's not happy.

THIRTEEN:

ETHAN

*Y*our timing is horrible.

All Mum wants to do is yank me out of the room as fast as possible, in case Violet infects me with I-don't-know-what — the Black plague?

Very funny, Violet think-says, and I realise I've just made what Rawiri calls a dad joke. I'd laugh if I weren't so pissed off at my mother.

'Ethan,' Mum says, barely acknowledging Violet. 'It's time to go home.'

Violet's distress is navy blue with streaks of red. *I thought you said an hour.*

I thought so too. I give my mother a stony look. 'Can we have a few moments?'

'I'm in a five-minute park,' Mum says. It's crap, and we both know it. Like most of the population, Mum only ever uses fusion-powered Zubers. Only rich people own their own cars.

People like the Black family.

Hey, Violet think-speaks.

Sorry. I stand up. 'A minute, then. Is that too much to ask?'

Obviously it is, but Mum doesn't say anything else, just retreats and hovers in the corridor.

After drawing the curtain back around Violet's bed, I take my PA out of my pocket. 'I'll message you. What's your number?'

'Here.' Violet takes her PA off the bedside cabinet and bumps the end against mine. Now we're in each other's contacts. *I prefer this method of communication, though*, she adds.

Of course. We can try. I reckon we'll get better at it.

I hope so. And I really need to know about this other person. Who is it? Where are they?

I peer through a gap in the curtain. Mum is rifling through her handbag in a semi-aggressive way, unkind thoughts stomping through her head: *of all the girls for him to get involved with, if she's anything like her father, blah blah blah.*

She's in Room G. Audrey Spelling, I manage, before Mum says, 'Ethan, would you get a move on?'

'Coming,' I call out, before kissing Violet again. *See you soon. Promise?*

Cross my heart and hope to die. I give her an evil grin.

She gives me an evil grin back. *That's so inappropriate.*

'Ethan!' Mum's about to detonate. The last thing I want is another scene, so I leave.

We're halfway to the car when my contact with Violet begins to blur. By the time I've reached the car, she's gone, and it's just me again. It's the weirdest feeling, as if I've lost an earlobe or a finger.

No, more than that. Much more.

'So much for the five-minute park,' I grumble, once Mum has stowed my bag into the boot of the Zuber, a lime-green two-door.

'I don't think you should be associating with that family.' She shuts the passenger door in my face and strides around to the other side.

'The rest of her family weren't there, in case you hadn't noticed.'

Mum's lips are a straight line. 'You know what I mean.'

'Violet's nothing like her father,' I say, watching Mum program our destination into her PA. The Bluetooth map on the car's console lights up. *Time to destination, twenty-two minutes*, the automated voice announces. The locks slide into place and the car eases into the traffic, joining a line of mostly identical Zubers. Ahead of us is the Sun Tower. Half a kilometre high, it took five years to build, and made angry headlines for months when the prime minister announced it was going to house the new parliament.

The citizens of Wellington will never forgive us Aucklanders, I don't think.

'Are you listening to me, Ethan?'

I power my window down. 'Herd immunity,' I say, even though I've only been half-listening. I've heard this lecture countless times.

'That's right,' Mum says, as I watch the multicoloured drones whizzing above us, delivering mail and pizza and parcels from online stores to the people of Auckland. 'If you vaccinate enough people, then even if the vaccine is weak — like with polio — there will barely be any infected people around to pass on the disease to the susceptible people. That's how we managed to eradicate polio.'

'But it came back, right?' It's not really a question. We both remember Charlie Hampstead, the boy from my Year 6 class who rode home from school on his skateboard one day, and returned two months later in a wheelchair.

Mum's lips are so thin they're barely visible. 'Yes, because many parents chose to stop vaccinating their children. And now the public is even more suspicious of vaccines after the M-fever debacle.' Then she's off again, using words like *fake intel* and *conflicts of interest*. It's making my brain hurt, so I shut her out again and gaze out of the window at the gated community to my right, at the rows of houses with their solar-panelled roofs and Insta-Lawns. No one wants real gardens and lawns anymore, not with the shrinking rainy seasons and constant water restrictions. Mum says nearly everyone had a back yard when she grew up.

The Sun Tower is behind us now and is, somewhat ironically, blocking out the morning rays. I wonder what Violet's doing, if she's sitting in the sunny spot in the dining room. Or maybe she's sitting beneath the cherry tree in the courtyard, pink blossoms settling in her hair. I try reaching for her again, but it's no good. The low-level buzz I've been aware of ever since I emerged from my coma is gone.

Once Mum is distracted with merging onto the Ring Road — she's been paranoid since someone's Zuber broke down a few months ago, causing a ten-car pile-up — I take my PA out of my jacket pocket. There's a message there already. How did I miss that?

I found Audrey, but she won't talk to me. Did she talk to you?

Not for long, I type back, and follow that up with, *Did you see her?*

No, I just . . . found her. You know.

I *do* know, and I'm feeling suddenly, inexplicably, jealous.

I miss you already, I write.

54

Violet's reply doesn't come until twenty minutes later, by which time we're nearly home. *I need to talk to you. Are you alone?*

Ten minutes, I reply.

I guess I must have been smiling, because Mum glances at me and says, 'No place like home, huh?'

'No place,' I say, but all I want is to be with Violet.

Not want. Need.

I was dreaming if I thought I'd get to call Violet as soon as I arrived home, though. As soon as the Zuber stops in our driveway, the front door opens. Freddie leaps across the Insta-Lawn with his usual five-year-old exuberance. Lyndall follows behind him, her legs looking even skinnier than usual in purple tights with a white bubble skirt over the top.

'Hi,' I say, scooping Freddie off his feet and putting him down almost as fast. I may be getting stronger every day, but I'm definitely not up to holding twenty kilos of kid for more than a few seconds. I turn to Lyndall next, who overcomes her usual thirteen-year-old aloofness long enough to give me a suffocating hug.

'Welcome back, Bill,' she says.

'Thanks, Jill,' I say, countering with *her* nickname, and we grin at each other. God knows how we came up with those nicknames, but they've stuck.

'Are you still infectious?' Lyndall asks.

'Would I be here if I were?' I pivot, filling my lungs with the spring-fresh air. OK, so it *is* good to be home. My legs are feeling wobbly, though, so I sit on the lawn while trying to make it look as though that's what I intended to do all along.

Mum's not fooled. 'Are you all right?'

'Dew, heavenly dew.' I lie back, emitting an *oof* when Freddie jumps on top of me. Mum doesn't say, *you'll catch your death of cold*, because she's a nurse and knows that viruses cause colds. Smiling, she carries on inside, my bag over her shoulder. I tussle with Freddie for a minute or so before getting to my feet and walking into our house.

'Come see our room!' Freddie tugs me down the hallway. We've been sharing a room ever since Lyndall pulled rank because she's a girl. Apparently she needs privacy now that she's a teenager.

I halt in the doorway. 'Ooh, balloons.' There are at least thirty of them bobbing over the floor and beds, blue and white and red, along with a heart-shaped balloon on the ceiling that says *So sorry you're leaving!*

'They ran out of *Welcome Back* balloons,' Lyndall says behind me.

'I was thinking you'd recycled the one from when you thought I was going to die,' I say, and am shocked to see her eyes fill with tears.

'I was *joking*,' I say, when Lyndall takes off into her room.

'She's a bit sensitive at the moment,' our mother says. 'Do you want anything to eat?'

'No.' I sink onto my bed. 'Actually, I'm really tired. I might have a nap.'

Freddie bounces at the foot of my mattress. 'I'm going to have a nap too.' Yeah, right.

'Let's leave your brother alone for a bit,' Mum says, hustling him out of the bedroom. 'You can play with Ethan later, OK?'

As soon as the door closes behind them, I call Violet. She answers before the PA has even started ringing.

'Are you at home?'

'Yeah, and I'm covered in balloons.' I laugh, but she doesn't join in.

'Hey.' Her voice is low and urgent. 'I think . . . I'm pretty sure they know.'

'They?' I sit up, pushing my hair out of my eyes. 'Who are *they*?'

'The doctors,' she says. 'Zelda Glass came to see me about half an hour ago. She asked if I've been hearing anything unusual.'

My heart begins to thud. 'What did you say?'

'I said no, of course. But I don't think she believed me. Audrey must have said something.'

'Crap.' I try to think back to the exchange I had with Audrey, but it was so brief, because she was like a scared rabbit. We said hi, and exchanged names, and that was basically it. I didn't have a chance to tell Audrey to keep quiet, to warn her about the dream that maybe wasn't a dream. 'What else did Doctor Glass say?'

'She just said, *I think it would be best if we scan your brain before you leave, to make sure there hasn't been any permanent damage.* She called it a NET scan. Do you know what that is?'

'I have no idea.' I've heard of a PET scan, a special kind of CT scan, but a *NET* scan? 'When are you having that?'

'Tomorrow.'

'Do you still get to go home?'

'I don't know.' Violet's voice is wobbling now. 'What if they decide to keep me in for more tests?'

'Look,' I say, with a certainty I don't feel, 'we're probably just being paranoid. This isn't something you can *see*, right?'

'I guess.'

'It'll be OK,' I say. 'Just let them do the scan, and then you can go home. And deny everything. Let them think Audrey's a nutcase. I mean, why would anyone believe her?' I don't know why, but I'm too scared to say words like *telepathy* in case the wrong person hears them. In case someone is listening over the network. In case someone else is able to listen in the way Violet and I can.

My heart gives out an extra-hard thud, so powerful I put my hand to my chest.

'Ethan? Are you still there?'

I clear my throat. 'Yeah. Hey, you'll be fine. But I'd block Audrey from now on, if I were you.'

My door swings open, making me jump. It's Freddie, in a cape.

'*Jesus*, Freddie,' I blurt.

'You're not asleep, you tricker,' my brother says, whirling around, his arms outspread.

'Do you have to go?' Violet asks.

'For now,' I say resignedly. 'Talk to you tonight, OK?'

'Tonight,' Violet says. 'Um, Ethan?'

'Yeah?' I stick a finger in my ear, the one without the earbud. Pity I can't block out my brother's babbling the way I can block out other people's thoughts.

'I hope we can . . . you know. Again.'

I don't have to read her mind to know what she's referring to now. Remembering the way her lips felt on mine, her breath in my nostrils, I smile.

'Me too,' I say. 'Talk tonight.'

FOURTEEN

VIOLET

fter lunch I do a circuit around the ward, trying not to think too hard about the scan I'm having tomorrow. Instead, I focus on placing one foot in front of the other. If I keep improving at this rate, I'll be able to drive soon. If I can drive, then I'll be able to borrow Mum's car to visit Ethan without forking out for a Zuber.

The ward is shaped like a hub, with a central nurses' station and a corridor coming off each corner. There are all sorts of obstacles to dodge along the way, like Robo meal trolleys and empty wheelchairs and the automatic drug-dispensing machine, which does the rounds at least four times a day. I don't mind. It's more interesting than sitting inside my room, staring at the images of Auckland trundling across the screen on the wall.

As I'm walking up the last of the four corridors, I slow and glance inside Room G. It's Audrey's room, which she shared with a ninety-three-year-old lady recovering from a stroke. The empty bed confirms what I already know, because her electric hum went silent a couple of hours ago. Either Audrey has gone home, or she has been taken somewhere else.

Maybe she went for her NET scan. If she did, then she's clearly not coming back, because there's no trace of Audrey in the room — the top of the bedside cabinet is empty, and the bed has been neatly made with hospital corners, as if she were never there.

The white-haired lady near the window gives me a crooked smile. It's crooked because only half of her face moves, due to the stroke paralysing the right side of her body. In a previous life, she was a foreign correspondent. I know these details because I'm shamelessly accessing her memories. War zones, cobblestone streets, terrorist attacks, a lover whose name she never knew.

'Gone,' she says. 'Gone.' A more recent memory flashes before me. It's of a slight girl who I know must be Audrey, sitting in a wheelchair propelled by a blank-faced orderly. Audrey is wearing yellow pyjamas with black Scottie dogs on them.

She went home in her pyjamas?

'Gone,' the woman says, and the memory dissolves. This lady used to have so many words, but now most of them are locked away, inaccessible to her.

'I know,' I say. 'Thanks.' I start moving again. I've taken five steps, maybe six, when I hear an unfamiliar voice.

'Violet,' it says. 'There you are.'

I look up. Standing in the doorway to my room is a short man who looks about the same age as my dad, early forties maybe. He's wearing a chalk-white suit and a digital stethoscope around his neck.

'Violet,' he repeats, before holding out his hand to shake mine. 'Let me introduce myself. My name is Doctor Noel Marlow, and I'm a neurologist.'

'Hi,' I say, even as a voice inside me screams *run run run*.

A wheelchair bumps against the back of my legs. I sit down with a thud.

'Don't be afraid,' Doctor Marlow says, and why can't I read him? Why?

I am very, very afraid.

I am being wheeled down a long, windowless corridor, Doctor Marlow striding beside me. The orderly pushing me is the same one who took Audrey away. He is thinking of his afternoon coffee break, and wondering if he's got enough time to make it to the VAPEX up the road to replenish his Vape juice supply.

Doctor Marlow's mind is a steel trap. I've tried once, twice, three times to access it, but I'm not getting anywhere. How can that be?

'Here.' Marlow halts and pushes on the wall. At least, I thought it was the wall but now I see a door swinging open. The neurologist steps to one side, beckoning us through. 'Welcome to my lab.'

The lab is almost as sterile as the corridor. A large, white machine emerges from the wall opposite the door, like a reptile from a cave. A bed lies in front of it, on what looks like a track that leads straight into the belly of the machine. Waist-high benches line the walls. On top of the benches sit various items of equipment — so far I've identified a tendon hammer and what looks like a glow-in-the-dark torch. But I have no idea what the other things are — heart monitors? Brain monitors? Instruments of torture?

'Do my parents know I'm here?' I wrap my arms around myself.

'Of course,' Marlow says smoothly. I have no way of telling

if he's lying or not. 'I advised them that we would like to conduct a neurological examination and scan before you go home tomorrow, to ensure there has been no long-lasting damage from the M-fever virus.'

Fixing my gaze on the machine, which I guess must be the NET scanner, I say, 'I thought that was tomorrow.'

'No time like the present.' Marlow's voice is crisp, with impatient undertones. 'I'm sure you'd like to get away as soon as possible in the morning.'

I'm sure I would, I think, but clamp my lips shut. *Just get it over and done with, will you?*

There's a hiss of doors opening, and a female nurse appears through another hidden entrance in the wall to my right. She's wearing green scrubs and a super-fake smile beneath her orange lipstick.

'Hi, I'm Francesca.' She holds out a blue gown. 'I'm going to help you get changed.'

'I don't need help.' I glare at Marlow. 'I would like some privacy, though.'

'Of course,' he murmurs, before disappearing through the automatic doors. The orderly has already gone, leaving me alone with Fake Francesca. After waving me towards the bed, she draws the curtains around. I undress as quickly as I can, leaving my underwear on. I've barely finished when the nurse reappears to fasten the ties on the back of the gown.

'Up here.' Francesca helps me onto the bed and pulls a blanket over my exposed legs. 'You need to take your earrings off. You can put them in here.' She passes me a small white pottle.

I finger my moon and star earrings, last year's birthday present from Celeste. 'Why?'

'Because it might scatter the images on the scan.' Francesca sounds impatient.

I've barely had time to access her mind — and she's thinking of how she'd love a coffee, God, does anyone focus on their job around here? — when I hear Marlow's heels clicking over the floor.

'I'm sorry if this is all a bit intimidating for you,' he says, his fingers curled around a metallic instrument with a bright light on the end. 'But you see, we've been very interested in the effects of M-fever on the brain. There are some patients who have reported that their brains work . . . well, better than before. Have you noticed anything different?'

I shake my head. *Ethan, Ethan, are you there? I know you said it was going to be OK, but I think you're wrong.*

Silence. I wish I hadn't left my PA in my room. I wish I hadn't agreed to accompany this man into the bowels of the hospital. What was I thinking?

'Hmm,' Marlow says, before proceeding to shine the light in my eyes, tap my elbows and knees with the tendon hammer and asking me to stick out my tongue. He even gets me to spell 'world' backwards, and subtract sevens from one hundred, all of which I do perfectly. After that, he sits on the end of the bed, an ankle crossed over his knee.

'Tell me, Violet. Did you happen to meet a patient called Audrey Spelling this week?'

'No.' I hope he hasn't noticed my split-second hesitation. 'I don't know anyone called Audrey.' My eye is caught, suddenly, by what appears to be a hearing aid in his right ear. He seems too young to be needing a hearing aid, but what do I know?

'Funny,' he says, his tone conversational now, 'because she

seemed to know all about you. How about a young man called Ethan Wright, did you meet him?'

I frown at him. 'Yeah. But he went home. This morning.'

'You two got to know each other quite well, didn't you?'

I shrug. 'Not really. We only met a few days ago.'

He holds my gaze. 'This may sound silly, but Audrey seems to think that the three of you could communicate in strange ways.'

'She sounds nutty to me.' My heart is tripping along, faster and faster. 'I never sent her any messages. I didn't even know her name until you told me just now.'

'But you know of her?'

My voice rises. 'I told you I didn't.'

Marlow gives me a faint smile, leans back slightly. That's when I see the screen above his head; why didn't I see it before? Maybe because it was turned off. It's playing a movie. In the movie, a couple are lying on top of a bed in a dimly lit room, kissing. They look strangely familiar, like a memory, and now I know why because—

'You filmed us,' I blurt. Oh God, why did I have to say that? Because now he knows, he knows . . .

The screen goes blank, and Doctor Marlow rises to his feet.

'So, Violet,' he says, 'shall we start again?'

And I open up my own mind as wide as I can, and try out my very first virtual scream.

Ethan. Ethan, if you're out there, I need help. Right. Now.

I am not afraid. I am petrified.

FIFTEEN

ETHAN

Mum makes green spaghetti for dinner, my favourite. It's an effort to eat tonight, though. I keep fiddling with my earbud, which I've set to verbally transmit any messages coming through on my PA, since Mum doesn't like us using devices at the table. I haven't heard from Violet since our conversation this morning, despite all my messages to her.

I'm figuring that either (a) Violet's PA is flat/broken, (b) Violet doesn't want to talk to me (Have I pissed her off? She didn't sound annoyed with me this morning), (c) Violet is sick with some sort of M-fever relapse (Does that happen? How would I know?), or (d) something more sinister has happened.

Lyndall waves in front of my face. 'Hel-lo, anybody home?'

I focus on her. 'I'm here.' In the periphery of my vision, I catch the worried look on Mum's face, and manufacture a smile. 'I was zoned out in spaghetti heaven.'

'There's plenty more,' my mother says. 'Help yourself.'

The food I've already eaten is a congealed mass in my gut, but I don't want to tell her that. I pat my belly.

'I'm good. Think Freddie's got his eye on the rest of it,

anyway.' I gesture at my brother, who has practically inhaled the contents of his plate already.

Freddie springs up. 'Yes, please.' He's so skinny; I don't know where all his kilojoules go. Probably he uses them all up because he never sits still. I touch the earbud again before taking it out to check the battery hasn't gone flat.

Yeah. Right.

'Ethan.' Mum's on me already. 'You know how I feel about tech at the table.'

'Sorry.' I take my plate out to the kitchen, feeling tired and agitated at the same time, a weird combination.

'Awesome.' Lyndall, standing at the sink, shoves a tea towel at me. 'You can dry.'

'Ethan needs to rest,' Mum says from behind me.

'I can sit on a stool while I dry.'

She shakes her head. 'Go rest in the lounge. You just got home today.'

'Make the most of it, slacker,' my sister calls after me. I stick my arm behind my back and extend my middle finger, which earns me a painful tea-towel flick behind the knees. It makes me smile, though. Life is starting to feel a little more normal.

Except, why isn't Violet responding to my messages?

After fetching my PA from my room, I flop onto the couch and say 'Screen on'. The wall in front of me lights up, taking me to a palm-tree-lined beach, where a pair of bikini-clad girls are trying to make a fire by rubbing sticks together. Ugh, it's *Teen Island*, the stupid reality show Lyndall's always watching. That's her main life goal at the moment — to end up as a *Teen Island* contestant. I speak into my PA again. 'Four News.'

It's just gone seven pm, but to my surprise, the M-fever

epidemic isn't headline news. It isn't even the second news item, which is about endangered bananas. Whatever. I don't care about bananas, which, at fifteen dollars each, are ten times the price of a measly apple. I want to know how many more kids have died. I want to see if there's any mention of kids with altered brains.

There's a thud from the kitchen, and loud crying from Freddie.

'You pushed me over,' he wails.

'Did *not*,' Lyndall bites back.

'Would you two stop?' Mum sounds tired, exasperated. Slumping into the couch, I examine my PA again. I feel a jolt in my chest when I see a new message, followed by a surge of disappointment when I realise it's from someone other than Violet.

Rawiri: *Heard you're out of prison, want to hang?*

Normally I'd be keen to hang out with Rawiri. Not tonight, though. I'm tired, and I'm worried.

Me: *Yeah, want to come around tomorrow?*

Rawiri: *Sure. You're going to love what I've done with our game!*

I'm about to compose another reply — something that sounds more enthusiastic than I feel — when I hear *M-fever*. Glancing up, I see that the news is finally reporting on the virus that nearly killed me.

'Health authorities say that there have been no new cases of M-fever reported in New Zealand for the past week,' the newsreader, a woman with marshmallow-plump lips, says. 'Caleb, do you think we can safely say the epidemic is over?'

The second newsreader, who is wearing an emerald-green dress that matches their dyed beard, says, 'We're daring to think that may be true.' Their goatee quivers with enthusiasm. 'Moreover, our investigative reporter, Simba Mason, has been speaking with a local scientist, who tells us that the reports of severe illness in those infected by M-fever have been greatly exaggerated. We're cutting to Auckland now . . .'

'*Exaggerated?*' My mother says behind me. 'You've got to be kidding.'

'Mum, I'm *listening*,' I say, my eyes fixed on the screen. Oh great, they're talking to *him*, eye-wateringly bright in a canary-yellow suit.

'. . . Doctor Nicholas Black,' Simba Mason says. They're standing on what looks like a helicraft landing pad at Auckland Hospital, the wind swirling their hair around their heads.

'He's not a medical doctor,' Mum shouts at the e-screen.

'*Mum.*' I turn up the volume. Mum emits a low growl and sits in the armchair, twitching.

'Unfortunately, we've been subject to a dangerous example of trial by media,' Black says smoothly. 'The Black study showed the vaccine to be effective in ninety-nine percent of healthy human volunteers, with no serious side-effects. Although the vaccination schedule for the general public hasn't worked out quite as well as we'd hoped, the post-marketing data has shown that we have successfully prevented infection in at least thirty percent of children.'

Simba Mason arches her sparkly eyebrows at him. 'That's quite a large discrepancy, ninety-nine percent compared with thirty percent. Some would say that the data from your trial on healthy human volunteers was seriously flawed.'

Nicholas Black holds up a hand, the sunlight flashing off his chunky rings. 'Not flawed, no, but the experience with the general public just shows we need to perform more research. Hence our application for another research grant.'

My mother's mouth forms an outraged O.

'What, so you can flush more taxpayers' money down the toilet?' she explodes, just before Violet's father starts going on about the dangers of blocking further research on a life-saving vaccine, and the risk of the clusters of M-fever escalating to a pandemic of COVID-19-like proportions.

'What makes you think he's lying?' I ask.

Mum's face hardens. 'Creating a vaccine in six months is virtually impossible. And as for his data on the healthy volunteers, I don't believe that for one second.'

Before I can ask her why that is, Freddie hurtles in and jumps onto my lap.

'Gotcha!' He flings his arm around my neck. I laugh and start wrestling with him. By the time I've forced my little brother off me, Mum has disappeared, and the newsreaders have moved on to the antibiotic-resistance crisis, which would be less of a crisis if the drug companies weren't charging such crippling prices for their new and improved antibiotics. Next is the latest terrorist attack. An ordinary-looking businessman strolled into a mall in London and blew himself up earlier today, killing six and injuring many more.

It's a shame these sorts of attacks are now so commonplace that they're the last item before the sports news, but there has been at least one a week since the immigration laws across the UK and US were made stricter a few years ago, meaning they basically don't take any refugees, and are sending a whole bunch of first-generation immigrants back to the famine-stricken, war-ravaged countries they were trying to escape in the first place. I decide to turn off the e-screen before Freddie starts asking questions I can't answer, like *Why do some people want to kill other people?*

'Do you want to play a game?' Freddie asks the second the screen goes blank.

I stretch. 'You know what? I'm pretty exhausted. I might have an early night.'

'It's only seven-thirty,' Lyndall says from the doorway.

'I know. I'll try and be less like a granddad tomorrow.' I sit up.

'You can sleep in my room this week,' she says. 'Until you feel a bit better.'

'Really?' I'm about to refuse, but I'm craving some time to myself, especially after a week with Eighties Music Freak.

'I changed the sheets on my bed,' she says, before sitting on the couch and turning the e-screen back on so she can watch — you guessed it — *Teen Island*.

In Lyndall's room, I strip down to my boxers and t-shirt and slide beneath the covers with my PA and earbuds. After selecting my music — Watermelon, of course — I surf the net for links to the M-fever epidemic. There are reports of ninety percent mortality from M-fever encephalitis, lots of them. But the more I look, the more I see that there are just as many reports countering those facts, saying the epidemic is propaganda, manufactured by pharmaceutical companies and scientists and doctors getting kickbacks off the same companies — scientists like Nicholas Black.

Vaccines contain heavy metals that lead to increased rates of dementia, autism, infertility and cancer, one link says. *If you care about your children's future, stop pumping poison into them*, says another.

I don't know what to believe. All I know is that Violet and I are living proof of what happens if you get M-fever . . . or are we? When I think back to that, it all starts to seem like a dream. Perhaps it never happened. Perhaps I was still delirious.

I slip my PA under my pillow and close my eyes, drifting on the surface of sleep. A young woman with short blonde hair and a spiral tattoo on her left shoulder is sitting on a swing. I'm on a swing opposite her. Higher and higher we pump, her iridescent green eyes locked on mine. She's chanting something, over and over, but the language is foreign to me.

Lauf. The word swirls around me. *Lauf, lauf.* And now her pupils are growing larger and larger, spirals drawing me in until something, *someone*, jerks me awake.

Ethan, Ethan, are you there?

My eyes fly open. *Violet?* I sit up, my heart beating like a metronome. The low-level hum is back. Violet's heartbeat is running alongside mine, two beats to my one.

Ethan, she repeats. *I'm in a car with no windows. They're taking me—*

Her voice cuts out, and the hum stops as abruptly as it began. My heart is a lone drummer once more, beating so fast it's a drumroll in my ears.

Violet! I think-shout. *Violet, if you can still hear me, don't give up, do you hear me? I'll find you, I promise.*

I sit up and stab *lauf* into my PA. The translation blinks up at me: *run.*

Run. Run, run.

SIXTEEN:

VIOLET

'm sitting in the rear seat of a car with no windows. For the past twenty minutes or so, we've been turning lots of sharp corners. I've been in this car for at least an hour, maybe more, ever since Doctor Marlow told me my brain was in serious trouble.

What sort of trouble? I'd asked. Marlow was still blocking me, his innermost thoughts a blank. While I was wondering how he knew to do that, he'd flashed up images from the NET scan on a tablet: slices of my brain. He'd pointed out a green glow in what he said were my temporal and frontal lobes, as well as my hindbrain.

The M-fever virus is still there, he'd said. *If we don't eradicate this for you, then you'll start to suffer hallucinations, seizures and, ultimately, death.* He'd looked very intently at me. *I suspect you are having hallucinations already.*

I'd stared back at him. Hallucinations? Was that what had been happening to me? But how could Ethan and I be having the same hallucination? Unless . . . What if Ethan was an elaborate figment of my imagination?

'Relax,' Marlow had said, his voice gentle. 'We can help you.'

He'd said I was to be transferred to a hospital with a specialised neurological facility. He'd said my parents would meet us there.

Now I'm wondering why I didn't put up more of a fight, why I didn't demand to speak to my parents straight away. I think it might have had something to do with the pre-med they injected into my vein before the NET scan, which had me fighting to stay awake.

But now it's worn off, and I'm more terrified than ever.

There's a panel dividing the driver's seat from the back seat, so I can't tell who is driving. Who knows I'm here? My parents? I doubt it. Zelda Glass? Surely she knows Doctor Marlow took me off for more tests — but what if she doesn't?

In desperation, I open my mind as wide as I can, and for the first time since Ethan left (could it have only been this morning?), I feel a slow, steady heartbeat threading between my own panicked staccato.

Ethan, I think-yell as the vehicle slows and comes to a halt. *I'm in a car with no windows. They're taking me—*

The door next to me is flung open. I barely have time to register the building in front of me — a dark-brown, circular structure — before a syrupy voice says, 'Welcome, Violet.'

It's a very tall black woman in a purple leather jumpsuit with a spiral emblem embossed on the left breast. She's wearing an earpiece just like Doctor Marlow's.

Ethan's voice reverberates around my skull. *Violet, if you can still hear me, don't give up, do you hear me? I'll find you, I promise.*

And I don't know what happens then, not exactly, but I feel a sharp pain in the back of my hand and everything goes blank.

I'm swimming through an ocean lit up like the night sky, with glowing coral planets orbited by phosphorescent fish. The sea is bath-water temperature and silky soft. Jellyfish undulate past, coloured pink and blue and green. I turn somersaults, one-two-three, before whizzing past basalt cliffs in the current.

As I pass over a crevasse, I slow down to peer inside and see an elephant with its trunk raised. An elephant? How the hell is that meant to breathe underwater? For that matter, how am I breathing underwater without a—

The image dissolves, and I'm jolted awake. Awake! Opening my eyes, I'm aware of my lungs first (and I'm breathing, just air, only air), followed by gravity weighing on my limbs. When I stretch out, my fingertips touch the head of the bed, my toes the other end.

Wait. I swivel my head from side to side. I'm in a bed, but not just any bed. This one has curved sides, and is alabaster-white. When I touch my chest, I feel rubbery, circular pads.

Beep. Beep. Beep. Someone's heartbeat. *My* heartbeat.

That's when I realise where I am.

The pods. Ethan's dream.

Not a dream.

Oh. No.

I try to sit up, but almost immediately a warm, heavy feeling begins to spread up my arms, through my chest, and into my struggling brain.

Relax, Violet, a voice says. It's the dark-skinned woman, I'm sure of it. Her name is Melody. She works for an organisation called the Found—

I fight, but it's no good. I'm being sucked under.

Here we go again.

74

SEVENTEEN

ETHAN

i sleep badly, flitting in and out of dreams. There's only one that stays with me when I wake the next morning. In that dream, I'm swimming through an ocean brimming with glow-in-the-dark creatures: jellyfish and coral and seahorses. In that dream, I can hear two hearts once more.

Violet, I dream-think. *Violet, Violet.*

She's with me, I know it, but for some reason she never replies.

When I slope into the kitchen, Mum is sitting at the table, dressed in her nurse's uniform.

'There's porridge in the pot.' She doesn't look up from her newspaper. My mum must be one of the few people in the world who still reads a print version of the news, although it's not the same news most people read online. Mum has an alternative newspaper called *The Rag* delivered once a week. She doesn't trust the mainstream hubs.

After pouring porridge into a bowl, I add sliced Fej-Apple and a dollop of yoghurt. My appetite has returned and it's bigger than ever, as if every cell in my body needs to catch up on all the food I missed out on.

'Make sure you check your email this morning,' Mum says when I join her at the table. 'The teachers have been sending through course notes and assignments.'

'Uh-huh.'

'Are you listening?'

'I'm listening.' I shovel porridge into my mouth. 'It might take a while to catch up on five weeks of missed school, though.'

Mum folds the newspaper in half and pushes it aside. 'As long as you make a start.'

'I will.' I don't tell her Rawiri is coming over this morning. What she doesn't know won't hurt her. I glance over at a half-visible headline on the paper, which is reporting on the latest outbreak of malaria in Queensland. 'Do you think we'll ever have malaria in New Zealand?'

'It's only a matter of time,' Mum says.

'Pity all those bush fires over there don't kill off the mosquitoes as well.' Mosquitoes and cockroaches will be all that's left if there's an apocalypse, I reckon, although I guess humans are part of malaria's life cycle, so maybe not.

Freddie bursts into the room, wielding a toothbrush. 'Mum, when are we going to Pedro's house?'

'In ten minutes.' Mum stands up. 'Freddie's going to spend the day at Pedro's. I'll pick him up on the way home from work. Can you make sure Lyndall spends some time on her schoolwork, too?'

'Sure. Although they'll be opening the schools again soon, won't they?' I give her a sarcastic shrug. 'Since the epidemic is over and all.'

'Don't hold your breath,' Mum mutters, before dumping her cup in the sink.

I tug *The Rag* towards me. The headline says: *Epidemic? What epidemic?* The sub-heading, in smaller letters, says: *How M-fever's victims are being covered up . . . in more ways than one.*

A cool trickle winds down my spine. I read on.

We've been asking doctors and nurses to anonymously report M-fever cases to our reporters, and the figures from around New Zealand will shock you — at least five dead for every one reported in the media. A virologist, who wished to remain anonymous, says, 'The current strain of M-fever is more virulent, more toxic than the measles virus most of us were vaccinated against as children. Ten percent of those affected develop encephalitis, an inflammation of the brain, compared with 0.1% of those affected last century. Of those afflicted with encephalitis, only five percent survive. This latter figure may be an overestimate. More worryingly, the eagerly awaited M-fever vaccine rollout has been a spectacular failure.'

'See you.' Mum surprises me by kissing me on the cheek. She gestures at the paper. 'You might want to pay some attention to that.'

'I don't need a newspaper to tell me M-fever can kill you.' I push it aside. Freddie thunders past, yelling 'Bye, Ethan', and I smile.

When the door closes, I go to my room and lie on my bed. Close my eyes. Open my mind as wide as I can, searching for Violet.

Nothing. Nothing. Nothing.

Either she's too far away, or she's unconscious or in a coma.

Or worse. I don't want to think about what worse might be. A new fear strikes me: what if the people who took Violet away are coming to get me too? I get up and touch the button on the window frame, activating my virtual blinds so that no one can see in but I can still peer out. All I can see are a pair of kids whizzing down the middle of the street on e-skateboards, and a couple of Zubers parked up at the Zuber stop. Nothing out of the ordinary.

But still, my heart won't slow.

A couple of hours later, Rawiri and I sit in the lounge, waiting for our VirtReal headsets to charge up. We're tucking into a Meatlover's pizza, which the Virtual Pizza Shack drone dropped off a few minutes ago. It's not real meat, which most people have given up now, but the advertisements would have you believe the taste is no different.

'So what's so great about this new game of yours?' I bite down on my pizza wedge. Breakfast seems like a very long time ago.

Rawiri nudges a crumb out of his Elmo-red fringe. 'I think you mean *our* new game.'

I frown at him. 'Seriously? I thought that'd be months away.' We've been working on Eternity for the past three years, ever since I dreamed up the idea while I was meant to be doing my maths homework.

'Me too, but then the schools closed. Not that I've finished the whole thing, but I've completed the first stage.' Rawiri peels his jacket off, revealing the Rod of Asclepius tattoo on his right bicep, a twin of mine. 'I need more story from you.'

I swallow. 'I've been otherwise occupied, in case you hadn't noticed.'

'A coma's no excuse. You could have dreamed up more plot while you were vegetating.'

I grin. Rawiri has what my mother calls a one-track mind. It's why he's so good at designing computer games.

'OK, smartass, show me what you've got.' I place the helmet on my head and pull the goggles over my eyes.

'Here goes.' I'm hearing Rawiri's voice through the helmet now. Almost simultaneously, my tinted view of our cluttered house disappears. 'Choose your character.'

'Coming right up.' It's not really a choice. I made up the characters, after all, while Rawiri's been bringing them to life. Using the touch screen, I skip over icons until I reach a tall, muscular guy with a dragon tattoo on his back. The dragon's wings spread across the shoulder blades look mean as. One day when I'm brave enough, I'm going to get a tattoo just like that.

Rawiri grunts. 'I knew you'd go for Roman.'

'And I knew *you'd* put big-ass breasts on your favourite character,' I counter.

'Her name is Venice, you sexist pig.'

'Whatever.' After arming myself with a bow and arrow, I select a shield and an ebony-coloured horse. 'Seriously, this is awesome, dude — I mean, Venice.'

Venice purses her lips at me. 'I know.'

'Stop it.'

'You love it.' Venice leaps on top of her trusty steed, a unicorn with silver eyes. I don't really need to see the preamble, since I made up the plot, but I read the words scrolling past me anyway, to make sure Rawiri hasn't screwed anything up.

The year is 3032. In a parallel universe not too far from here, a pair of renegades are setting off on a mission to free the Dragon Queen from her prison high in the Citadel of Cirrus. The Dragon Queen's healing powers are desperately needed to save the children from certain death by a plague that only affects those who haven't yet reached puberty — and prevent a whole tribe from being wiped out. However the Queen's captors, the Meth Heads, are the most feared of all tribes, as they are stir fucking crazy.

'Did you have to put "fucking" in there?'

'I can delete it if it offends your delicate whatevers, Wright.'

'Later. And it's Roman.' I set off down a tree-lined path to my left, and Venice jogs her unicorn into a canter. The imagery is pretty damn good. Screw school, Rawiri and I could make billions with this.

Then I feel guilty for enjoying myself while Violet is — what? What is she doing, and where? Why am I playing VirtReal games when I should be looking for her?

The next thing I know, I'm sprawled in the dirt, a pair of giant hawks whirling above me.

'Damn, you're an easy target.' Venice lets loose a flurry of arrows at the hawks — with her left hand, because all Rawiri's characters are left-handed, just like him. 'You'll be dead before lunch time at this rate.'

'That was almost painful,' I grumble, getting to my feet.

By the time Rawiri leaves, it's nearly four o'clock, and we've completed the first stage of our game. A Zuber pulls into our driveway only a few minutes later. Mum is in the front, with

Freddie bouncing in the booster seat behind her.

Freddie runs into the lounge and announces, 'Ethan, I learned a new song,' before regaling me with a song about a dance where everyone starts sneezing and falls down.

'That's not new,' I tell him. 'It's a song about the plague.' I haven't heard that nursery rhyme since I was a little kid.

Freddie's brow wrinkles. 'What's a plague?'

I'm about to tell him it's when your skin turns black and falls off, but remembering how I made Lyndall cry with my *sorry you're leaving* balloon joke yesterday, I just say, 'It's like having a really bad cold.'

'The plague, the plague,' Freddie yells and takes off down the hallway.

I raise an eyebrow at Mum. 'Maybe it's a remake. The "Ring-a-ring o'roses" song, I mean.'

Mum gives out a short laugh. 'I'll be sure to tell the team tomorrow.' She surveys the lounge. 'Looks like you got lots done today, then.'

'I've been very productive.' I nudge an empty pizza box beneath the couch with my foot. 'How was your day?'

'You don't want to know. Gosh, it's dark in here, how do you stand it?' She goes to open the virtual blinds.

'No, don't,' I say quickly.

She frowns. 'Why not?'

'The light's kind of hurting my eyes today,' I say, casting a nervous glance out into the street. There's a black 4WD parked across the road that I don't remember seeing before. What if it's *them*? And who are *they* anyway?

'Are you all right? Do you have a headache?'

I duck before Mum can plant her palm on my forehead. 'I'm

fine. My eyes have just been a bit sensitive since I got sick,' I say, right before Freddie runs in and jumps on my lap, clutching a box of crackers.

'Not before dinner,' Mum says, and Freddie starts moaning, so I retreat to my room for some peace. I lie on my bed, intending to close my eyes for just a minute . . . one minute . . .

I'm flying. I never knew this could be so easy, am not sure why I've never tried before — over the houses in my neighbourhood, huddled close together, above the tail of the Whangaparāoa Peninsula and over the shimmering ocean. In the distance the Sun Tower, rising high above the city, glows golden in the late afternoon light. I fly above the Harbour Bridge with its rows of Zubers and Fuse buses and Lightning scooters, branded drones zipping around me.

As fantastic as the view is, there's only one thing I'm interested in right now. I'm seeking that second heartbeat, the intoxicating yellow sunshine of her, just her.

Violet, where are you?

Surely I can't be dreaming, because I can hear Violet now. She's so loud I don't know why I didn't hear her before.

Ethan . . . is that you?

After swooping over the Waitematā Harbour, I veer towards the Waitākere Ranges.

Keep talking, I say, even though I've figured out that she doesn't really need to anymore. Her blood is coursing through my ears. Her breath is in my lungs.

Ethan. Her mind is a tangerine flare. *I knew you'd find me.*

And *there*, deep within the mānuka and pine, nestled amongst the punga and ferns, is a dark-brown building with a central hub and spokes radiating around the periphery. My belly clenches when I see the uniformed sentries strolling around the perimeter. The weapons slung across their backs don't look like toys. Yet when they look up, their eyes pass over me as though I'm not even there.

Violet says, *Don't forget this, Ethan. And by the way, going back hurts like hell.*

And then — snap! *Jesus.* I curl into a ball on my bed, clutching my belly. When I breathe it's as if the air has blades in it.

But something has happened, something good — because as faint as it is, I still have Violet's heartbeat in my ears.

I touch the tattoo on my arm. Think of dragons and citadels. Think of my new brain, and my new heart.

No time for sleep. Not tonight.

EIGHTEEN:

VIOLET

It's Thursday, and my second day at the Foundation. I've finally been released from my pod. My arms and legs are stiff, as if I've run a marathon rather than floated in an in-between world while doctors and scientists monitored changes in my brain activity. They put me through a series of challenges, until I didn't know what was made up and what was real. Mazes made of hedges, and confidence courses with rope swings across raging rivers, and spiral stairs carved into sheer mountains, along with intellectual challenges — riddles and algebra and logic problems that became so complex I wanted to scream.

Which answer is True? Which is False, and which is Random?

Rules and questions, questions and rules. I know they want me to think outside the rectangles and squares they've put me in, but I can't, I can't.

I don't know. I don't know, I don't know.

But I have a secret, a ray of hope. Ethan found me today, and I found him — deep within my brain, his heart beating in my chest, his breath whistling through my nostrils.

Just after he left (but not really because we have a thread

between us now, thin and yet as strong as silk), an alarm sounded. A young doctor came to check on me, her pupils wide with worry. After shining a light in my eyes, she asked me to repeat words after her, just like Zelda Glass did last week.

'What are you looking for?' I asked.

The woman hesitated. 'There was . . .' She looked over her shoulder, then back at me. 'Some unusual activity before. On your scan.'

'In my temporal lobes?' I asked.

Her mouth fell open. 'How did you know that?' She was thinking about how medical school hadn't prepared her for this. She was hoping I wasn't going to die on her.

Die on her? As soon as I tried to work out why she might be thinking that, my limbs and head grew heavy again. When I came to, I don't know how many minutes or hours later, Melody was lifting the lid on my pod.

'Are you hungry?' she asked.

Not surprisingly, I'm starving. I'm sitting by myself in a small, sterile-looking room with a table surrounded by four chairs. Everything is white, apart from the cannelloni and salad.

For the first time since I've arrived, I'm in a room with a window. All I can see in the fading light is thick vegetation, the trees so tall I can barely see the tops of some of them. If I didn't know better, I'd think they were kauri, but they're nearly extinct after the dieback went crazy a decade or so ago. Perhaps, after Melody sedated me the first time, they took me up north, where the last of the kauri reside in protected forests. But that would mean Ethan and I can communicate across hundreds of kilometres. Could our range really have expanded so far in so little time?

My stomach churning, I push my plate aside and run my fingers over the shiny white jumpsuit that Melody gave me to change into. At least it's less revealing than the hospital gown. But I want my own clothes back. I want to go home. How long are they going to keep me here? What if they never let me go?

I cast around for Ethan. *Are you there?*

He doesn't answer, but I can still feel him, can sense his colour, navy blue streaked with silver. Is it that we're getting stronger, or is he physically closer to me? Perhaps he's projecting himself again, the way I projected myself earlier today — hovering above my prone form for a few seconds before jerking back into my skin, painful electric shocks radiating through my body.

By the way, going back hurts like hell.

Is this hell?

The door swings open. It's Melody, clad in the same purple jumpsuit all the staff here seem to be wearing. 'Would you like anything else?'

I scowl at her. 'I want to speak to my parents.'

She closes the door and sits opposite me. 'I know you do, but it's really important we finish our assessment first.'

'Do they even know I'm here?'

'I know this is hard,' she says. 'But if we don't finish our assessment, then both you and your parents could be in danger.'

I cross my arms. Melody is blocking me. I want to find out how she does that, just like Doctor Marlow.

'You've kidnapped me,' I say. 'And drugged me. You've experimented on me without asking for my consent.'

Her hand darts across the table, her fingers encircle my wrist. 'Violet.' Her voice is low, urgent. 'You have to understand. This is a matter of national security.'

It sounds so corny I almost laugh, but when I catch the expression on her face, I realise she's actually serious. The rage bubbling inside me is almost too great to contain.

'Let go of me,' I say. 'Or you'll regret it.'

Melody releases me, her block slipping for a moment. I hear *what if* and *abilities we don't know about* before the wall is up again, more impenetrable than ever. That's when I realise that she has no idea what I'm capable of.

That makes two of us.

Rubbing my wrist, I say, 'Is this room bugged?'

'Bugged?' Melody fingers her ear, touching the hearing aid that I'm pretty sure isn't a hearing aid. 'I don't know what you mean.'

I force a note of steel into my voice. 'I know when you're lying. So don't even try.'

Her eyes flicker. 'All right, then. This conversation is being recorded. What else do you want to know?'

'How many others like me are you holding here?'

She tilts her head, as if listening to whatever is coming through her earpiece. 'Five of you,' she says, after several long seconds.

'What are their names?'

'It's not important for you to know that.'

'You've kidnapped me and it's not important for me to know?' I want to rip the earpiece out and stomp on it, but I'm pretty sure that will only result in me being forcibly restrained. 'Am I allowed to meet them, or are you going to keep me in solitary confinement?'

Melody frowns. 'You're not in solitary confinement. And you will meet them in time, but we have a few more assessments to carry out first.'

'You call drugging me and monitoring my brain an assessment?' I push harder and sense a wobble in her shield. 'Audrey,' I say, plucking the name from the forefront of her consciousness. 'Phoenix. Harper. Callum.'

Melody leaps up, knocking her chair over. 'Sedate her, *now*!' she yells.

'No.' I clutch my arm, clawing at the implant nestled beneath my skin. It's no good. The drug is working already, sucking me under. If only I could figure out how they keep—

'Have a good sleep,' Melody says, before stepping forward to catch me.

Bitch.

NINETEEN

ETHAN

While the rest of my family are settling into bed and going to sleep, I'm doing anything but. In the privacy of my room, I lay out black trousers, a long-sleeved top and hiking boots. In my schoolbag, I pack a bottle of water, a waterproof jacket, a loaf of bread, chocolate and dried apples. At the last minute, I add the headlamp I use when I go mountain biking at night. Checking my bank account on my PA, I see I haven't got much money, but enough to buy more food for the next few days if I need it.

I don't know how long I'll be. I'm not even entirely sure where I'm going, but I'm pretty sure if I concentrate, I'll be able to find Violet. It reminds me of a game I used to play with Lyndall when we were younger, yelling out 'warm' or 'cold' if we got closer to or further away from hidden objects.

After placing the backpack beneath my bed, I turn off my light before opening my virtual blinds. The street is quiet, no people around and barely a drone in sight. Hardly a surprise, since it's nearly eleven pm. And yet . . .

The black 4WD has returned. It disappeared around dinner

time. I know, because I've been checking ever since I first saw it. But it's there once more, sitting across the side of the road like a shiny fat slug.

I climb into bed, fully clothed, and draw the covers to my chin. Outside, a car door slams. I hold my breath, listening.

I'm being paranoid.

I'm being stalked.

Footsteps, getting closer. Jesus, they're right outside, slapping a path to our front door. Panicking, I slide out of bed, grab my boots and backpack and sprint down the hallway, reaching the back door just as someone starts rapping on the front one. *No, no, no.*

I fling open the door, my heart screaming in my ears, and dash across the lawn and through the gap in the fence to the next property. Crouching by the side of the house, I hear voices. One of them belongs to my mother, the other to a woman I don't recognise.

'Hello?' Mum sounds very alert, rather than as if she's just been woken from sleep. Very alert, and very suspicious.

'Hi,' an unfamiliar voice says. 'I'm very sorry to disturb you so late, but I'm from the Public Health Department. It's about your son.'

'Which one? I have two sons.' I sense the fear coursing beneath my mother's steely exterior. She's thinking, *But both my boys are safely asleep . . . aren't they?* I shove my feet into my boots and lace them up with shaking fingers, listening intently.

'I'm referring to Ethan. I'm sorry to visit this late, but we've just received some disturbing information.'

'You — what?'

'Some disturbing information,' the woman repeats, as if she's reading from a script. 'I'm very sorry, but we need to detain Ethan under the Public Health Act. We have reason to believe he may still be infectious and a danger to others.'

I don't wait to listen further. Instead, I race across the lawn before exiting onto the street behind, where I run towards the nearest Zuber. As the car pulls away from the kerb, I think-say, *Are you awake, Vi?*

No answer.

I'm coming to get you, I say, stretching out on the rear seat so that no one can see me. *Hang in there, OK?*

I don't know if what happened earlier today was a dream or true astral projection, or whatever it's called. I don't have any other clues as to where Violet is, though, so I instruct my Zuber to take me to a Super Mall out west, which is so big it even has its own traffic lights. It's half-past eleven, so everything is closed. Never mind. I didn't come to shop.

Once I've exited the Zuber, I lurk in the shadows of the hulking edifice and tune into Violet again. Her signal is definitely stronger. No doubt she's asleep, which accounts for the swirly dream images; too hazy for me to make out. I think about projecting myself again, but I need somewhere safer than outside a mall in the middle of West Auckland.

Violet. I hate to wake her up, but I don't really have a choice. *Can you hear me?*

Almost immediately there is a yellow flare inside my head, as if a match has been touched to a wick.

Ethan, oh my God, where are you?

Take a look. I stand up and start strolling around the complex — past the shops selling shoes and luggage, past the

Natura-Medical centre, past the beauty parlours with their advertisements for rainbow eyebrows and Total Laser Therapy for everyone's unwanted body hair and freckles and I-don't-know-what-else. Electronic billboards morph as I stroll past, their facial recognition software communicating with marketing algorithms to tempt me with advertisements for e-skateboards, zit cream, i-shoes with built-in running soundtracks.

Turning away from the nearest billboard, which is lecturing me on safe sex, I say, *Do you think this is anywhere near you?*

You're closer than before, for sure. I sense the purple edges of her panic. *But you need to be really careful. They keep sedating me by activating an implant they put in my arm while I was unconscious. If they catch you—*

They won't catch me, I think-say, blocking her from my memory of the so-called Public Health employee banging on our door, while trying to hide my horror at the thought of someone implanting something in Violet's body without her permission. *Have they hurt you?*

No . . . I get a sudden, blinding surge of terror, and then it's gone, as quickly as it came.

Are you sure? I've got a feeling similar to when I stuck a knife in our toaster as a kid, and got an electric shock.

I'm not sure. Her thought-stream quivers. *Nothing hurts now. Maybe it was just a nightmare.*

You're in one of those pods, aren't you? I wander through the car park, which is empty apart from an abandoned SUV in the far corner. From the looks of the twisted fender, it's probably not going anywhere any time soon.

Yeah. They've been giving me challenges, making me solve problems and mazes and things.

I tug the zip on my jacket up to my chin, wishing I'd worn an extra layer. *Can they tell you're talking to me now?*

I'm not sure. They're monitoring the activity in my brain, so maybe they'll see my speech centres light up. She hesitates. *Ethan?*

Yeah?

Have you been keeping up with the news?

Sort of. Why? I don't really have to ask. I'm already seeing an image of her parents: Nicholas Black in his bright red suit, her mother in a white linen dress.

No, I think-say as gently as I can. *There haven't been any news items about you going missing.*

Have there been reports of anyone *missing?*

I'm getting their names now: *Phoenix. Harper. Audrey. Callum.*

I don't think so. I didn't see the news tonight, though. Violet's right. How it is possible for five teenagers to go missing without the media getting hold of it? What if the next headline is 'Missing, presumed dead'?

Oh. God. Violet's colours have morphed from yellow-purple to indigo-black.

Sorry. I'm sure they haven't been saying that.

But what if they have?

Then they're wrong, aren't they? Violet's not dead. And neither, I realise, as the collective hum within me grows, are the others.

Violet's new fear is big and scarlet and almost painful.

No, I say. *No, why would they do that? They're testing you for a reason.* Last night's dream-image looms before me, unbidden: the girl with the spiral eyes, telling me to *lauf. Run, run.*

But what if they realise we're of no use to them? Violet asks. *What then?*

Well . . . I rub my own arm in the exact spot where I can

feel Violet's implant irritating the tissues beneath her skin. *Then they'll let you go . . . won't they?*

No, she think-says. *No, they won't.* She's thinking lethal doses of sedative. She's thinking of how easy it would be to dispose of bodies in the depths of the forest. I'm seeing super-tall trees with massively wide trunks. I wonder if she has any windows where she is, or if the image is something she's conjured from memories.

Violet, don't. Anyway, it doesn't matter, because guess what?

Violet's colour changes again, hints of light blue diffusing through.

You're coming to get me, she think-says as if it's a fact, right before her brain shuts down. For a moment I panic, until I realise I can still hear her heart. It's beating a little faster than before, but it's still strong, still steady, still alive.

For now. I need to get moving, and fast.

I hurry back to the SUV and use the torch on my PA to examine the interior before trying the driver's door. It's locked. So are the passenger doors.

After dumping my bag on the ground, I peel off my jacket and wrap it around my right fist until it resembles a warped boxing glove. Then, praying there are no security guards or police drones in earshot, I punch the rear window as hard as I can.

I never really needed a word for my soul before now. I guess I didn't truly believe I had one, being brought up on a diet of scientific fact.

If I had to give my soul a word, I'd call it my dream-flow, the place where dreams are made.

My sluggish, inconvenient body is lying on the rear seat of an abandoned SUV in the mall parking lot. The essence of me, my dream-flow, is hovering high above the mall. I'm turning towards the collective hum, towards Violet's heart. Travelling downstream, a river to the sea.

Violet Black, here I come.

I'm flying, across houses and roads, up into the hills, above the trees, rātā and tawa and kahikatea. Violet's blood surges in my ears, a waterfall. Softer, but just as strong, I hear the hearts of the others, too. I feel the wind of their breath licking my cheeks.

Us. We. The collective.

I needn't have worried about finding them. When the sound of their blood is ocean-loud, I halt, floating above the hub-and-spoke building *they* call the Foundation. My dream-flow takes in the security guards with their semi-automatic guns and Dobermans, the electric fences with killer voltages, the automatic gates that provide entry from the road.

I've found you, I send to sedated-Violet. *I've found you, and I'll return soon. I promise.*

I follow the road upstream all the way back to the mall, so I can remember where I will need to drive in the morning. Back to the car park, back to the corner where the SUV is parked.

Where the SUV *was* parked.

All that is left in the parking space is shattered glass.

The SUV is gone.

So is my body.

TWENTY:

VIOLET

O n Friday morning I wake smiling, as if I've just had a delicious dream.

A dream that wasn't a dream.

I've found you, and I'll return soon. I promise.

He was so close, but not close enough. Still, I felt him, sensed his dream-flow.

'Dream-flow.' I roll the words around my tongue like a boiled lolly. Ethan's word, not mine, but it's perfect.

'Violet.' It's Melody, wearing her purple jumpsuit uniform with the spiral on the left breast. 'How did you sleep?'

I sit up, shoving aside the blanket that is fashioned in the exact shape of my pod.

'Why do you even ask? You know exactly how I slept.' I wave at the monitor behind me, the one with images of my brain on it. My temporal lobes glow purple. My frontal lobes are yellow. I have no idea what it all means.

Melody's expression is blank. 'It's polite to ask, isn't it?'

Clamping my lips together, I take in the cigar-shaped boxes attached to the walls. There are at least ten of them, maybe more, and they're as big as the front fenders on the Zubers that have taken over our city.

'What are those for?' I point, wondering why I haven't noticed the objects before. I guess I was too distracted, or too drugged.

'They're part of the scanner.'

'The NET scanner?'

Melody's lips curl upward. 'This whole room is the scanner. We call it the WEB. It makes the NET scanner look pretty amateur, when you think about it.'

Not wanting to think about it — as if I could do anything about it, anyway — I gaze down at my horrid hospital-issue pyjamas, pass my fingers through my lank locks. 'Can I have a shower?'

'Of course.'

'How about a trip to the gym?' I don't even bother to hide the sarcasm in my voice. *Or a trip home, how about that?*

To my surprise, Melody says, 'Yes, why not? It would be good for you.'

Sarcasm gets you everywhere.

I'm sure Melody is buttering me up before she socks me with something else — as in another dose of horse sedative, followed by more mind-bending challenges — but I'll take what I can get.

This morning I take a long shower, after which I'm given a brown paper bag with a clean white jumpsuit to change into. This one is made of some kind of stretchy material, with short sleeves and a spiral over the left breast, identical to the logo on Melody's jumpsuit. The spiral creeps me out, but I'm not sure why. At the bottom of the bag, I find a pair of white socks and white leather trainers with green soles. When I turn the shoes over to get a better look at the soles, I see that they're patterned with spirals too.

Definitely creepy, I think, before sending the image to Ethan.

I don't get a reply, but I can hear his heartbeat. It's rapid, as if he's running.

Are you OK? I think-ask.

Still no answer, and then Melody is back to distract me with breakfast — quinoa porridge with cashew milk and maqui berries, accompanied by the most delicious smoothie I've ever tasted.

'Blueberry and banana,' Melody says, sitting opposite me. We're in a different room to last night, but the view out of the window is the same. Trees. Ferns. Men with guns. Wondering if the guns have spirals on them, I choke back a laugh.

Melody, for the first time since I accessed the names of the *others* from her mind, looks concerned. 'Are you allergic?'

'I don't think so.' I take another sip, trying to remember when I last had a banana. On my seventeenth birthday, I think, when Dad splashed out on deep-fried bananas at a fancy restaurant. As for blueberries, even my father doesn't earn enough to source those. 'Where'd you get them, the black market?'

'You don't need a black market when you work for the Foundation.' She taps her metallic purple fingernails against her front teeth. 'After you've had your workout, I'll chat to you some more about that.'

Work for the Foundation, is she kidding? I want to go to the gym, though, so I swallow my sarcasm, along with the rest of my endangered fruit.

The gym is at the end of a very long corridor lined with multiple doors, all of them closed. The door to the gym is closed too, but it opens when Melody presses her thumb against a touch pad to the left of the door frame.

'Open sesame.' She steps aside to let me enter. At first glance, it's a standard-looking gym, with weights, rowing machines, exercycles and treadmills. It's not until I climb onto an exercycle that I see the helmet.

Melody slips the helmet off the handlebar. 'Put this on.'

'I'm not going to fall off.'

'It's not to protect you. It'll add a whole new dimension to your workout.' She smiles. 'I promise.'

I don't trust Melody, if that's even her real name. I'm curious, though, so I take the helmet and slip it onto my head. Melody slides a pair of goggles over my eyes.

'Start pedalling,' she says. 'That'll activate the helmet.'

I start pedalling, and as I do, the sterile walls of the gym disappear. I'm cycling along a mountain-bike track in a forest with very tall, gnarly trees. Large, interlacing tree roots snake beneath the forest floor. As I keep riding, I get more confident and start jumping over the raised tree roots. The more I do that, the larger and higher the roots become.

Another challenge; I should have guessed. But it's kind of fun. I'm not even tired, despite this being the most exercise I've had in weeks.

The forest floor begins to slope upward, until it becomes so steep I'm worried I'll fall off the bike if I don't keep moving. Of course, none of this is real . . . or is it?

The scenery is different now, more like native bush than something out of a fantasy world. The koru in the ferns are like the spirals on our uniforms, on the shoes I'm wearing.

My thighs are burning, my breath short. I take a deep breath, and that's when it hits me — the scent of damp soil and rotting leaves. This is taking VirtReal to the next level.

At last, unable to pedal anymore, I plant my feet on the ground before climbing off the bike. I reach out a hand to touch the moist trunk of a punga tree, but I feel nothing.

Perhaps that's because I don't have a hand. Or a body, for that matter. When I look around, the bike has disappeared.

All I have is my dream-flow.

Yes.

A voice drops into my ear. 'Violet?'

Snap. I'm lying on the floor of the gym, my knees drawn up to my chest, my eyes watering. Waves of nausea undulate through me. Does it get worse, the further you get from your body?

'Violet? Sorry, I should have made you stop.' Melody is crouching beside me. 'Did you black out?'

I stare at her, at Melody's memory-image of me falling sideways off the exercycle. 'No,' I manage, after she takes her fingers off the bounding pulse at my neck.

But it wasn't my own heart I heard thundering in my ears, right before I left the VirtReal world.

It was Ethan's.

TWENTY-ONE

ETHAN

Words can't describe the panic I'm feeling. I've lost my body. I don't know how I can even be me without my body. I'm a floating consciousness, an abstraction of thought.

In the minutes after I realise the SUV has been driven away with my body in it, I swoop around the mall in useless circles before widening my search. I pass houses, a block of shops, a rest home: all of them in darkness. *Concentrate, concentrate.* But how can I concentrate when my heart is beating so fast?

Wait. My heart. I can hear it, getting louder and louder the further I get from the mall. And now I'm approaching a large building, or rather a set of buildings, with signs saying *Hospital* and *Emergency Department*. There are two ambulances parked outside. As I pass one of them, I sense a residue of me inside: shed skin cells and I don't know what else. That's not what's pulling me on, though — not even close.

And then *whack*, I'm curled in a ball, my mouth opening and closing like a fish. I twist away from the sudden light but it follows me.

'Pupils equal and reactive,' a man says. I squeeze my eyes shut and feel warm fingers on my cheek. 'Can you hear me?'

'I can hear you,' I whisper, still clutching my belly.

Going back hurts like hell.

It does, it does.

'Can you tell me if you've taken anything? Pills, alcohol?'

I open my eyes. Stare at the man, who has a bushy black beard and a stethoscope around his neck. 'No.'

'What about needles? Have you injected anything? P, heroin, Q?'

'No, nothing.' As if I'd go anywhere near Q, which makes P look like candy.

Black Beard takes a mini-Tab off the end of the bed and taps on the screen. 'Have you had any episodes like this before?'

'I don't think so.' The pain in my stomach is receding. I'm thirsty, and inexplicably hungry, considering it's still the middle of the night. At least, I think it is.

'Any medical history? Seizures, recent bumps to the head?'

I sit up. 'I had M-fever recently.'

'M-fever?' He shrinks away. 'How recently?'

'Weeks ago. I'm not infectious anymore.' I cough again, glance around. There are only two other patients that I can see, an elderly woman wearing an oxygen mask and a snoring man in the bed opposite me, his presumably broken leg encased in a glowing blue bubble-like case. 'What time is it?'

'Quarter past three.' The man, whom I assume is a doctor, gives me an intent look. 'M-fever, you say. Were you admitted to hospital?'

A curly-haired nurse approaches with an identical hospital-issue mini-Tab.

'I've found him,' she says. 'Ethan Wright, discharged from hospital a few days ago.' She deposits something on the cabinet beside my bed. It's my PA, with my photo ID clearly visible on the front screen. 'You were quite sick, weren't you?'

'I'm all right now, though. And I need to go home.' My mind races. 'I've got to look after my little brother when my mum goes to work today.'

Black Beard and the nurse exchange a look. 'Sure,' Black Beard says. 'But I suspect the police will want to talk to you first.'

'The police?' *Oh yeah.* There's the small matter of me breaking into an SUV. I wonder where it is now — with its owner, perhaps? Feigning ignorance, I say, 'Why? Blacking out isn't a crime, is it?'

Black Beard frowns. 'Tell me, Ethan, what's the last thing you remember?'

'I'm not sure,' I bluff. 'One minute I was falling asleep in my bed at home and then I woke up and I was here.'

'You don't remember breaking into an SUV? The owner got quite a shock when they returned to find a comatose teenager in there. You're lucky they chose to drive you here rather than to the police station.' Black Beard takes the torch out of the front pocket of his scrubs — not just any torch, but the type doctors use to look in people's eyes. After asking me to look up, down, and directly at the super-bright light, he says, 'Well, it all looks OK to me, but I'm going to give Neurology a quick call.' When I dip into the blue-green cloud of his thoughts, I pick up that he's worried that I've had some sort of seizure due to encephalitis. I guess, in some ways, he's not too far from the truth.

'But I'm fine.' I can hear my heart pounding in my ears, but from the inside rather than the outside. I never thought I'd be so happy to hear my own heartbeat. 'Does my mum know I'm here?' I look down at my bare chest, which is covered in sticky dots like the ones they used to monitor my heart when I was sick.

'I can call her for you,' the nurse says. 'The number's right here on your record.' She holds up the mini-Tab.

'I'll do that after I talk to the neurologist,' Black Beard says. 'Back soon, Ethan.' They exit the cubicle, leaving me to stare at the peaks and valleys on the heart monitor beside my bed. My heart is going one hundred beats per minute, and every now and then, there's a short run of peaks, like the Southern Alps. I'm trying to work out what that means — maybe it's something that happens to everyone now and then — when the nurse returns.

'We're going to transfer you to the neurology ward,' she says.

'What? Why?'

The nurse wraps a blood pressure cuff around my arm. 'The neurologist wants you to have a special scan of your head so they can try to work out why you had this episode.' And all I can hear is Violet's voice: *She called it a NET scan, do you know what that is?*

Trying to hide my rising panic, I say, 'Are you going to call my mum now?'

'We'll make sure to do that,' the nurse says, but when I reach into the surface of her consciousness, I hear the whispered conversation she had with Black Beard only minutes before.

Probably best if we don't call the mother yet, at least not until he's had his scan. We don't want her to panic.

'OK . . .' *Think, think.* 'Um, can I go to the toilet?'

'Sure.' The nurse unhooks me from the blood-pressure cuff and gives me a hospital pyjama top, blue with a V-neck. 'It's just to the left of those double doors down there, see?'

'Sure, thanks.' When I reach the toilet, I turn to see the nurse adjusting the elderly woman's oxygen mask. The automatic doors, sensing my presence, have slid open — so I walk quickly through them, my eyes straight ahead. If only I'd thought to ask for my shoes, but that would have looked suspicious. I stop to remove my socks before hurrying to the end of the corridor, through the next set of automatic doors and out into the crisp black air. Picking up the pace, I break into a jog when I see the hospital gates in front of me.

I've barely made it onto the street when I feel a piercing pain in the side of my neck. Seconds later I feel something running through my veins, hot and heavy, *oh shit*, and I try to open my mind as wide as I can, *Violet*, but then my heart gives out an extra-hard thud and I'm

Falling

And I

TWENTY-TWO:

VIOLET

'Are you sure you're OK?' Melody asks. It's two hours since I fell off the bike, two hours since Ethan's heart moved back into my range. I'm lying on a bed in a new room, one with a view of the gigantic trees outside my window.

What have I been doing? Feigning sleep. Trying to reach Ethan. Failing to reach Ethan.

Are you OK?

No answer. Perhaps he's asleep. Perhaps he's unconscious, or drugged.

'Violet?' Melody says, and I realise I haven't answered her yet.

'Just a bit tired,' I say.

She gives me an intent look. 'Did anything strange happen in the VirtReal sim?'

'No,' I lie. 'I think all the moving around just gave me — what do you call it?' I spin my finger around my head to illustrate.

'Vertigo.' Melody seems disappointed. 'Are you hungry? I was going to take you to lunch, introduce you to someone.'

I swing my legs over the side of the bed. 'Someone?'

'He's been sick too, just like you,' she says, and I feel a jolt in my chest. Could it be Ethan? But he's not answering me, why? Have they done something to him? I try to get an answer from Melody's inner thoughts but come up with nothing. Either I've lost the ability to read people's minds, or she's become better at blocking me.

What if it's the former? Is that why I can't communicate with Ethan?

Frowning, I follow her down the shiny white corridor. We're walking in the opposite direction from this morning, away from the gym. After turning left, Melody leads me down another long corridor with a red door at the end.

'This,' she says, waving her hand in front of a sensor on the wall, 'is one of our cafés.'

'Café?' The door slides sideways into a cavity in the wall. I smell coffee, baking bread, bacon. But when I look inside, I see there's only one person in the room — a guy with silver-blond hair and a tattoo above his left eyebrow. He's wearing a white jumpsuit like me, and he's sitting on an electric-blue couch by the wall to my left.

Melody smiles. 'Come on, don't be shy. Violet, this is Phoenix. Phoenix, this is Violet.'

'Hi.' Phoenix doesn't smile. He barely even looks in my direction. If I had to guess, I'd say he was a couple of years older than me.

'Hi,' I mumble, trying not to stare at the tattoo, which looks like characters from a foreign language — Japanese? Mandarin?

'Just order what you like from the counter,' Melody says breezily. 'I'll see you in an hour or so.' Then she's gone, the door swishing shut behind her.

An hour? I sink into an orange armchair and swing my eyes around the room. It's circular, with a variety of differently coloured armchairs and couches around the periphery and a lozenge-shaped counter in the middle. I don't know how I'm meant to get anything when there's no one around to take my order.

'There's a tablet on the counter,' Phoenix says, examining his fingernails, which have been chewed to the quick. 'You just select what you want.'

I wander over. The tablet is built into the counter and lights up when I approach. I select a Triple Jack and waffles with banana and raspberries from the menu. I've never had so many bananas in my life.

'Money buys you everything.'

I spin around. 'What?' I ask, before realising he is a telepath, just like me. *Of course.*

Phoenix gives me a sardonic smile. *Of course*, he echoes, and I see how his eyes jerk upward. *Don't look now.*

They're monitoring us, right? I return to my chair.

Did you think they wouldn't?

I don't know what to think anymore.

It's the only weapon we've got, sister.

I sense the blue-grey eddy of his emotions, so strong, so powerful, that I feel my own answering surge of despair-hopelessness-grief.

I'm sorry, I think-say.

Everyone is. Phoenix springs up and paces the room. His memories of his younger sister are vivid and disturbing. Bloodshot eyes, an angry rash, blackened fingers and toes.

Hearing a whirring noise, I turn to see a shelf sliding out from beneath the counter, with a tray containing my Triple Jack and waffles. Looking away, I see that Phoenix has moved to the window.

What can you see? I ask.

What they want me to see. He turns around. *You don't think it's real, do you?*

Ignoring my lunch, even though my stomach is growling, I cross the room to stand beside him and peer out at the black-sand beach, the wild surf, the charcoal sky.

How do you know it's not real? I ask.

How do you know this isn't real? he counters. And now the sand is bleached-white, the water still and turquoise. I glance up and to my left, straight into a tiny lens mounted just below the ceiling.

Did they do that?

No, Phoenix says. *I did.* And then, *Don't look at me like that, Violet. Sit down and eat your food, and listen up.*

Part of me doesn't want to do what he tells me, if only because he's being super-patronising. But I take my tray and sit down like a good girl.

How long have you been here? I think-ask, stabbing my fork into a round of banana.

Four weeks. And I didn't mean to be patronising.

I roll my eyes at him. He rolls his eyes back at me. Stifling a smile, I look down at my food.

Listen up, he repeats, as if I have a choice. *Because we don't have long.*

I chew. Swallow. Listen.

Before I got sick, Phoenix says, *I was in the army.*

The army?

Don't sound so surprised. Keep eating. He's looking out of the fake window, which has morphed back into the West Auckland beach scene.

I sip on my Triple Jack. *As if they don't know we're talking to each other.*

As far as they know, I'm being sulky and non-communicative.

Big words for an army guy.

Phoenix drums his fingers on the side of the couch. *Now who's being patronising? Are you listening?*

I'm listening.

Well, anyway. My sister got sick so they kicked her out of her boarding house. I went home to look after her.

What about your parents? I ask, and there it is again, that blue-grey swirl. Sad, sad, sad; this is what it feels like to lose your whole family.

Helicraft accident two years ago, he says. *When Tilly was fifteen and I was seventeen.* He's stroking his left forearm. I'm guessing he's got an implant in there, same as me. *Anyway. She got sicker and sicker, and I took her to the hospital but she died two days later. A week later, I had a fever as well. The next thing I knew, I was in the intensive care unit. Three weeks of my life, gone. It was four weeks before I could walk without help. I thought I was going home. And then . . .*

He's showing me more images. Images of a pod, just like the one I've been sleeping in — except this is like Ethan's dream, the dream that most definitely isn't a dream — because there's more than one pod, and they're not empty.

The others, I say, the names springing, pre-formed, to the front of my brain: Harper. Audrey. Callum. *Have you met them?*

Only in here, he says, and I'm back in the underwater world with the fluorescent jellyfish and rainbow coral, but I'm seeing it through Phoenix's eyes. *And here.* Blink, and I'm running through a jungle, my heartbeat thundering in my ears.

No, not my heartbeat. Phoenix's heartbeat.

Not just my heartbeat, he think-says, and now I know why his heart sounds so loud.

Phoenix-Harper-Audrey-Callum, I say.

And you, he says, and I can hear all of them now — not just them, *us*, our hearts beating in synchrony — *Violet-Phoenix-Harper-Audrey-Callum*, sixty beats per minute, tick-tick-tick. But something, someone, is missing.

Ethan, I say. *We have to find him.*

The door slides open and Melody flashes her teeth at us. 'Have a nice chat?'

Phoenix springs to his feet and pushes past her without a word. At least, not to her.

No, he think-says, as he moves away. *Not we, you.*

'I don't think he likes me,' I tell Melody. When I reach for Phoenix to see what he thinks of that, he blocks me, quick as lightning.

Bastard.

I heard that, he says, and then he's gone. Gone, but not gone.

Tick. Tick. Tick.

TWENTY-THREE:

ETHAN

I'm lying in a confined space. My wrists and ankles are restrained. When I try to move my head, I realise that's locked in place, too. The only body part I have control over is my eyes.

My eyes, and my mind.

It's dark. No, not completely dark. There's a glow from above me, a blue rim of light around the edge of what I'm guessing is the ceiling.

'Welcome, Ethan,' a measured voice says, and almost immediately, the restraints are released from my wrists and ankles, and yellow light floods into the room.

I sit up and look around, but there's no one to be seen. There's a camera, though, in the top left corner of the ceiling.

I glare at it. 'Too afraid to show yourself, are you?' Clutching the sides of my bed, I realise it's not really a bed at all. No, I'm in a pod, just like in my pseudo-dream — except there's only one pod in the room rather than rows of them. The only other objects I can spot in the room are large metal boxes fixed to the walls all around me.

'A temporary precaution.' The voice is male, smooth, almost

certainly private-school educated. There's a hiss to my left, automatic doors opening, and a man wearing a white suit strolls in. When I try to dive into his mind, I get nothing, a blank. My heart begins to race. Does that mean this man is like me, if he can block me like that? Can he read *my* mind?

'I'm not infectious anymore,' I say, and that's when I realise something just as scary as the man reading my mind, if not more so.

I can't hear Violet's heart, can't hear the collective hum. What's happened to them? What's happened to me? What if I've lost my newfound abilities?

Maybe it's a good thing. Maybe this man, whoever he is, will let you go.

But what about Violet?

'I know you're not infectious,' he says, approaching the pod. 'At least not in *that* way.' The man extends his hand. 'Welcome. I'm Doctor Noel Marlow.'

'Where is she?' I ask, ignoring his hand.

Marlow blinks at me. 'Where is who?'

'Violet Black.'

Sensing movement, I glance over his shoulder and see a pair of blank-faced men in black jumpsuits flanking the door. Marlow's brain may be a blank to me, but I'm accessing images from the man on the left. A comatose girl on a stretcher, a plane, what the hell? 'Where have you taken her?'

'You got that, did you?' Adjusting something in his ear, Marlow turns to smirk at the guards.

I leap out of the pod. Of course it's futile, but my blood is boiling, orange-red flares in my retinae, and I shove him hard and he stumbles and I'm expecting the guards to grab me but instead,

I feel a pain in my arm
   The implant
   And I scream *Violet*
   But of course she's
   So far away
   From
'Night-night,' Marlow says.

TWENTY-FOUR:

VIOLET

When I return to my room after meeting Phoenix, I see that a few items have been installed while I've been away. In addition to the bed, there is a blue desk with a red chair in front of it. Facing the window is an exercycle with a pair of VirtReal goggles hanging from the handlebars.

I step closer to the window and pick up the goggles. The trees outside look the same as before. The recent conversation with Phoenix niggles at me.

What can you see?

What they want me to see.

And then Phoenix had changed the view. But how? Squinting, I conjure up a memory of an island my family once visited in Fiji — golden sand, palm trees, a lagoon with turquoise-coloured water.

The gigantic trees begin to ripple and blur. I open my eyes wider. It's there. The island. The water looks so fresh, so inviting.

'Anything interesting out there?' It's Melody *again* — does she ever get any time off?

'I don't know,' I say, resisting the urge to shrink away when she comes to stand beside me. 'Perhaps you can tell me.'

Melody crosses her arms. 'We're lucky,' she says, 'to live in such a safe country, aren't we?'

Clearly she's not seeing the same tropical island as I am, but to test her, I ask, 'What kind of trees are those?'

'I don't know. Native bush.' She gives me a searching look. 'What kind of trees do you think they are?'

'Kauri,' I say, as my memory-image disappears, to be replaced by the same view as before.

The same view.

What can you see?

What they want me to see.

I clutch the VirtReal goggles. 'It's not real, is it?'

'What's not real?'

I wave the googles at the window. 'Everyone knows kauri are nearly extinct. How stupid do you think I am?'

'I don't think you're stupid.' Melody glances upward, and almost immediately the view morphs into something else.

Somewhere else.

'How about this?' Melody asks.

I stare at the brick-red soil, the low tussock, a bleached-white tree with no leaves.

'I don't know. Australia?' I ask, distracted by the sardonic voice slipping between my confused thoughts: *Did you think you were still in New Zealand, little Kiwi?* How long has Phoenix been listening to my thoughts?

'Shut up,' I say, before realising, in my panic, that I've spoken aloud. 'I mean, sorry, I don't know what I mean.' I sit on the bed and hang my head in my hands.

Melody touches my shoulder. 'Are you all right?'

Careful, Violet, Phoenix replies and then he's gone, sort of, but I can feel the collective hum deep within my chest. It's kind of reassuring.

Kind of.

'Fine.' I look up. 'You didn't answer my question.'

'Yes,' Melody says. 'Central Australia.'

'You've taken me to Central Australia?' But how do I know that this image is any more real than the image of native bush they were showing me before? How can I trust anything, anyone?

'We needed to keep you safe,' she says, and in my mind, the collective whispers, *don't trust her, don't trust her, don't trust her.* They don't have to tell me that. I already know.

'When?' I ask.

'We flew you out on Saturday.'

'Saturday? But it's Fri—' Wait. When was the last time she sedated me? How much time slipped past while I was under? I'd thought it was minutes, an hour at the most. 'What day is it now?'

'Sunday.'

I stare at her. How do I know she's telling me the truth? How do I even know I'm in Australia? I could be locked in an underground cellar in a back yard in New Zealand. I could be locked away in a remote part of the hospital, being fed a fake life while under sedation.

Violet, stop, Phoenix whisper-speaks. *Panicking is not going to help you. Tell her you want to meet the others.*

I open my mouth. I say, 'I want to meet the others.'

Melody examines the bleak landscape out of the window. 'Sure,' she says.

And, despite everything, despite how much I distrust and despise her, I feel a lurch in my chest. I think I know what that feeling is. I think it's called *hope*.

Hope is what we hang onto until our hearts stop beating. Once we lose hope, we die.

I don't want to die.

TWENTY-FIVE:

ETHAN

After twenty-four hours in the pod, drifting in and out of what I suspect are drug-induced dreams, I'm moved to a room with a single bed and a view. Out of the double-glazed window, I see pine trees, ferns, men with guns. *Welcome to the Foundation*, the German-accented assistant tells me on day two, when he hands me a white jumpsuit with a spiral on the breast. He tells me his name is Bruno. I tell him to piss off, and he does, but it's temporary. Minutes later, I black out, sedated by whatever has been released from the implant in my forearm.

On day three (I think it's Monday, but I'm not sure how long I was under the third time, after I told Bruno to piss off), I wake to an insane hunger. I'm dressed in the same underwear and long-sleeved shirt I was wearing the night I left home.

Hell, my mum will be going crazy with worry, not to mention Lyndall. I hope they've made up a convincing story so Freddie doesn't freak out too.

I leap out of bed and stride to the door. To my surprise, it slides open as soon as I approach. I've barely set foot in the long, featureless corridor when I hear a familiar voice.

'Good morning, Ethan. Looking for something?'

'I'm starving,' I say, after a brief pause where I consider (a) hitting Bruno and making a run for it, or (b) demanding I go home. Both options, I know, are futile, especially with this implant in my arm, so I opt for (c) cooperation. For now.

'I'm sure.' Bruno's voice is as smooth as his face. He's younger than Marlow, late twenties at a guess, with olive skin and a chin so smooth I suspect he's had his facial hair lasered off. Either that, or he's got some weird medical condition.

Weird medical condition, yeah, I can talk.

'I'll bring you a breakfast tray,' Bruno says. 'There's an ensuite in your room if you'd like to shower.'

'Mmph.' I stride back into my room/cell and shut the door. The ensuite is lined with shiny white tiles from floor to ceiling. I stare at my image in the mirror above the square basin, rub my bristly chin. My teeth feel gross, so I take a toothbrush out of the holder on the basin and apply a long stripe of toothpaste before scrubbing them as hard as I can. Then I stand under the shower for at least ten minutes, relishing the pounding of the water on my skin. If nothing else, at least I won't smell like a half-dead rat if I'm lucky enough to see Violet today.

And yet, something tells me Violet is no longer anywhere in my immediate vicinity. If she were, I'd be able to feel her. I can't feel anything, anyone. Not anyone like me, anyway.

Where have they gone? Are they dead? And what does that mean for me?

I'm blocking my own thoughts now. It's either that, or give in to the fear burrowing beneath my skin.

I am not afraid. I am not afraid.

Breakfast is better than I expected. Extra-strong coffee, a banana and blueberry smoothie, and pancakes with maple syrup, whipped cream and raspberries. I've barely finished eating when the door slides open and Marlow enters, flanked by the same blank-faced men who were with him on our last encounter.

'Hello, Ethan,' he says, as if I hadn't tried to attack him when we last met. 'Did you enjoy your breakfast?'

'I'd have enjoyed it more if I weren't being held captive,' I reply.

'Touché.' He sits at the chair beside my desk and crosses his legs. I don't know what touché means, and almost reflexively, I try dipping into his mind for a clue. Of course it won't work, I realise, and that's when I detect it.

It. A silver shimmer, so subtle I could almost have missed it if I weren't holding my breath.

Oh.

Marlow adjusts the ridiculous purple bow tie he's paired with his white suit this morning. 'Understandably, you must be getting bored. I have a few activities you may be interested in, designed to strengthen both your mind and body.'

'Sounds riveting,' I mumble. I push again, slightly harder this time, and the shimmer becomes a tantalising undulation. Thought fragments stream towards me, the signal so scattered I can barely make sense of them.

Conditioning. Intensification. Bavaria. The prototype.

'I know this is frustrating,' Marlow says. 'But we're here to help you realise your abilities. If we let you go home now, it could threaten your safety and that of others around you.' His thoughts are less shiny now, grey rather than silver, the colour of half-truths.

I lift my chin. 'Does my family know I'm here?'

Marlow's gaze is steady. 'No.'

'My mum will go to the police,' I say. 'She'll report me missing.'

'No,' he says. 'She won't.' And I'm hearing *relapse* and *quarantine* and *for the greater good*.

I clench my fists. 'You've lied to her, haven't you?' Marlow's eyes flare, and I realise I need to be careful. If he knows I'm accessing his thoughts, he'll find another way to block me, and then I'll have nothing, no weapons.

'Think of this as a Protection Programme.' He leans towards me. 'For you, and for your country.'

'My country?' I laugh, but stop when I realise he's not joking. He's not lying either.

'So,' Marlow says, his thoughts so slippery I can barely grasp them, 'do I have your cooperation or not?'

There is, I know, only one right answer.

TWENTY-SIX:

VIOLET

i don't get to meet the others straight away. No, first I have
two days of what Melody calls *preparation*. Preparation, or
assimilation? I don't know . . . yet.

On Monday, I'm subjected to a battery of tests. Blood tests,
another NET scan, an ECG reading of my heart. That afternoon,
I'm put through more challenges, mostly puzzles and logic
questions like the ones I was given last week at the Foundation.

'I've never been good at riddles,' I grumble to Melody. We're
sitting in a circular room with a circular desk. Even the seat on
my chair is round. At my right elbow is a jug of sparkling water
with strawberries and mint bobbing on the surface. At my left, a
bowl of chocolate-covered licorice balls. I can't fault the cuisine
in here, I suppose.

'Think laterally. Outside the square.' Melody is sitting on a
silver ottoman, a mini-Tab on her lap.

'There're no squares in here, only circles.' It's meant to be
a joke, until I realise that it could be true. I gaze at my oval-
shaped fingernails before swinging my eyes around the room.
Even the window is circular. Is this meant to be a joke, or

something designed to drive me crazy?

Melody taps the mini-Tab. 'Take your time.'

A hot mixture of frustration and resentment washes through me. If it weren't for the stupid M-fever, I'd be going about my usual business in New Zealand. It's Monday, so I'd be at school. I'm not sure what the time zone difference is, exactly, but perhaps I'd be in English, writing my essay on Atwood's *The Handmaid's Tale*. Possibly I'd even be sitting next to Jasper, because if it weren't for M-fever, he wouldn't have died.

But then you'd never have met Ethan.

Does meeting Ethan make up for being held captive by a bunch of psychopathic doctors in a desert?

Scowling, I stare at the problem on the mini-Tab in front of me.

> A king is celebrating his birthday in a few days. One thousand bottles of wine have been ordered for the party, and these arrive ten hours before the start of the party. Unfortunately one of the thousand bottles of wine is poisoned, but they don't know which one. The king decides to sacrifice a slave, but the poisoned wine will not kill the slave until ten hours after he drinks it, by which time the party will have started. What is the minimum number of slaves who will have to be sacrificed to find the poisoned bottle?

I hate this kind of problem. It ties my mind up in knots. And yet, something is flickering at the edges of my brain.

Think outside the square.

No, a voice think-says. *Think outside the circle. Get it?* It's Phoenix, his blue glow more obvious now.

Easy for you to say, I think-reply. *Have you tried answering these questions?*

Show it to me, he says. So I do, as best as I know how, my mind wide open.

Ah, he think-says. *You can use binary to solve this one.*

Binary? I have a vague inkling that binary is used for computer coding, but how does an army recruit know about that?

No need to be rude. Phoenix sounds amused rather than annoyed. Then he opens *his* mind, and I have no idea what a binary representation of integers means, at least not at first. But as his thought-stream mingles with mine, I begin to realise that maybe I'm not as ignorant as I first thought.

No, it's not that. I didn't know how to get to the answer before, and probably never would have by myself. I'm learning, but not in a way I've ever learned before. I can almost feel the neural networks forming and solidifying a new highway for my brain.

Oh, I say. *Wow. Thanks. But seriously, how come you're so good at maths?*

I'm not, Phoenix replies, and I'm getting a sense of someone else, but it's a memory rather than a presence. Phoenix's memory.

You accessed this off someone else, I say. *Didn't you?*

Survival of the fittest, he says, before blinking out, like a light bulb.

I type in the answer: *10*, and am rewarded with a *correct* flashing across the screen in hot-pink letters.

So simple, when you know how, I think. The collective hums. I move on to the next question.

After that, the rest, as they say, is history.

Melody doesn't comment on my perfect test scores. She doesn't tell me I can meet the others yet, either. The next afternoon, though, she takes me somewhere different.

Not *completely* different. I'm stuck inside the same air-conditioned building as before. Melody directs me into an elevator and presses a green button. When the lift opens, I see something completely unexpected through the automatic doors in front of us. The room is as large as the gymnasium at school, and is lined with a steeply banked oval track.

'A velodrome?' I ask.

'Correct.' Melody strides ahead of me and waves at the sensor beside the doors. 'Do you like cycling?'

'I fell off the last bike,' I remind her. Either she doesn't hear me, or she chooses to ignore me.

'Here,' she says, leading me to what appears to be an equipment and changing room. 'Choose a bike, any one you like.'

Just like a character out of a Doctor Seuss book, I think, and hear a low chuckle, internal rather than external.

Fancy meeting you here, I say. I could block Phoenix, I guess, but I'm too starved for company for that.

Wild horses couldn't keep me away, he banters.

It's a bike, in case you didn't notice.

Whatever. He retreats, although not completely, his presence a blue shimmer at the edges of my consciousness.

'Violet?' Melody gives me a weird look.

'I'll take this one.' I grab the first bike I see, one with a silver frame and red handlebars. I let her strap a helmet beneath my chin and try on a couple of pairs of bike shoes before finding a lime-green pair that fit perfectly.

I've never been in a velodrome before, let alone ridden in one. Guess there's a first time for everything.

I start off slow at first, but it's easier than I thought. It's not long before I'm whizzing around the track, leaning into the curves. My post-M-fever body seems to be more coordinated than the old one, now that I've recovered from my weeks of lying in bed. Is this another type of neurological assessment, or is it some kind of fitness training? Every now and then I glance up into the stands. Each time, I see Melody peering down on me, as if I'm the most fascinating object in the universe. Ugh.

There are no windows in here. But as I keep going around and around, my brain begins to wander, first figuratively and then literally. After a few minutes, the walls of the velodrome blur and disappear, and whoa, I'm somewhere completely different, somewhere I've never been before.

Welcome, Phoenix think-says, *to our world*.

I open my dream-flow. Let the world rush in.

It's red.

TWENTY-SEVEN:

ETHAN

On Tuesday morning, Bruno brings me a new set of clothes to wear. *This is more like it*, I think, as I slide my limbs into the shiny black trousers and a black t-shirt with a metallic-silver sheen. I'm given black trainers to match, with red soles. Every item of clothing has a spiral embossed on it somewhere, including the shoes. It's kind of weird, but better than a white jumpsuit.

After a breakfast of what I'm sure must be genetically engineered food — I haven't eaten honey since the bee vermin crisis three years ago — Bruno leads me into a large room with an exercycle in the middle.

'Do you like VirtReal games?' He gives me a helmet and a pair of goggles.

Giving him a blank look, I say, 'They're OK, I guess.' The less information he knows about me, the better, I figure.

'Just put the helmet and goggles on,' Bruno says. 'And start pedalling.'

It's a pretty ordinary simulation at first. I'm a mountain biker in a forest that looks very much like the one outside my window.

I progress through a series of challenges, each one harder than the last. The trails have names like Sidewinder and Descent of Death. The latter, admittedly, requires a lot more skill, but my reflexes are lightning-fast.

No, better than that. Perhaps they're not really reflexes when I already know what's coming — how does that work? No sooner have I asked myself the question than I have the answer: I'm accessing someone else's memory of this game.

Bruno, Bruno, who knew you'd be such an easy read?

Is that intentional, I wonder? Do *they* — whoever Marlow's colleagues are — intend for me to do that, or have I taken them by surprise?

No surprise if they don't know you're doing it, I think. I'm almost looking forward to my next encounter with Marlow, so I can pump him for more information.

The tracks keep coming, steeper and windier by the second, but it's no challenge when I know what's coming around the corner. Bored, I let my reflexive memory, if that's what one can call it, take over while I think back to the VirtReal game Rawiri and I are designing. It's so much more sophisticated than this. If only I were in Roman's VirtReal body right now, with my quiver of poison-tipped arrows strapped across my muscular back.

That's when something really weird starts happening. The pines and ferns give way to massive trees with gnarly trunks, and in the cloud haze above me, I see the glow of not one but two suns. The next thing I notice is that the motion of my bike has changed from a bump-bump-bump to a more rhythmic up-and-down motion.

Glancing down, I see that I'm no longer riding a bike. Instead, I'm sitting astride an ebony-coloured stallion.

'Arrow,' I whisper, and my horse whickers in reply. Faster and faster Arrow gallops, until we've left the forest behind. We race across the plains, Arrow's hooves leaving the ground for seconds at a time. His haunches are shiny with sweat. How is it that I've ended up in my own VirtReal game? Have the Foundation managed to gain access to it? But how? It's not even online yet, because we haven't finished it.

In the distance, I spy another familiar figure, and a very shapely one at that. Venice isn't looking too happy, probably because she's tied to the biggest tree I've ever seen, one with a jet-black trunk and a canopy comprised of dinner-plate-sized leaves. I recognise that tree, because it came straight from my imagination.

I halt in front of Venice, my breath fogging in the wintry air. 'Need a hand?' I dismount from my horse and slide a knife out of the belt around my waist

'Ethan, what the hell? Is that you?' The voice is low and sultry, Venice's voice, but the speech patterns belong to my best friend. Is this my own memory I'm accessing, or I am playing Rawiri in real time? And if the latter is true, can the Foundation see what I'm doing?

A third idea comes to me. But no . . . surely not? And yet, if this isn't a memory, and if Rawiri hasn't put our game online, then only one possibility remains.

I'm inside Rawiri's head.

TWENTY-EIGHT

VIOLET

On Wednesday morning, I wake with the feeling that I've been in dream-sleep, or what my father calls REM sleep, all night. Most of the dreams centre around the experience I had the day before.

This is what happened in the velodrome yesterday, or rather, what happened once I left my body. My dream-flow hovered above a solitary building in the middle of the desert. Unlike the one in New Zealand, this building was shaped as a spiral rather than a hub-and-spoke configuration, alabaster-white against a dazzling blue sky. I didn't look at the building for long, though. The scenery was flooding in, and it was red, red, red. Red rocks, red dirt, and in the distance, red mountains. As my body continued to spin around the velodrome, a reflexive action controlled from my motor cortex (and don't ask me how I know that, but I'm learning, I am), my dream-flow did the same around the building, my loops growing larger and larger.

I'm in the middle of nowhere.

We're *in the middle of nowhere*, Phoenix think-said. *Don't forget.*

Don't forget what?

A gigantic bird moved into my sphere, its wings beating the air.

About us. We're stronger than they think.

Speak for yourself, I thought-spoke, but I felt a new energy moving through me. I followed the bird, marvelling at its wing-span, which must have been at least two and a half metres across.

Wedge-tailed eagle, Phoenix said.

Ooh. Wondering how he'd managed to do that — project himself as a bird of prey, I mean — I swooped between a pair of termite mounds. Ahead I saw brick-red mountains, a gorge. *Are you coming?*

Right behind you, kiwi bird.

Kiwis can't fly, didn't they teach you that at school? I swept between the sheer cliffs, Phoenix's laughter trailing behind me like a jet trail. The water below was black, glassy, sinuous. I wondered if I'd see a crocodile.

Not here, he said. *Water monitors, maybe. And snakes. Look, see?*

He was right. A brown snake lay coiled on the rocks. It stirred as we passed, its head waving from side to side.

Do you think it sensed us? I asked.

Maybe, Phoenix replied. Before I could think too much about that, I felt the sickening pull that told me I needed to return to my body *right now*.

Go, Phoenix said, so I gave in to the tether and *whack*, I was lying on the floor of the velodrome, dry-retching.

'Are you all right?' Melody had asked.

'Never been better,' I'd replied.

This morning, Wednesday, I stand in my room, frowning at my smart mirror. It's showing me the outside temperature (twenty-five degrees), the weather forecast (a sun icon), and an image of snow-tipped mountains (as if). When I touch the mirror, the fake scenery melts away, leaving my reflection in its place. I've been given a metallic-blue dress to wear, one with the ever-present spiral embossed over the left breast. I slide my legs into the white leather boots someone left in my room while I was out and tug the zips to my knees.

What's next? A tiara? A sword? I smooth my hair, which is draping over my shoulders for the first time in years. I can't remember the last time I had it cut, but it was probably at least a month before I got sick. That was, what, eight weeks ago?

That seems like someone else's life now.

Is this a life?

I don't know, but I'm about to meet the others, the collective. A mixture of anxiety and excitement rolls within my belly. At least the nausea has passed. It's eighteen hours since I explored the stark world outside with Phoenix the wedge-tailed eagle.

The minute I think of Phoenix, a new feeling creeps in, one I have trouble identifying at first. Shoving it away, I try to summon a memory of Ethan. How long since we last communicated? Five days?

Ethan, are you out there? Can you hear me? Is it possible to communicate between countries, to reconnect across the Pacific Ocean?

There's a knock on my door. It's Melody.

'It's time,' she says.

Melody takes me to a room located at the end of the outermost arm of the spiral, at the opposite end of the building from my bedroom, which is tucked into the centre. The closer we get, the louder *they* are; a confusing cacophony of thought fragments and not-so-foreign heartbeats. Not so foreign because they've been with me for days now.

Welcome, Violet, one of them says before I even set foot in the room, and the others join in with *hi* and *hey*. Melody waves me inside.

'This is Violet,' Melody says to the others, who are sitting on a collection of couches and beanbags, as if in a high-school common room. 'You've met Phoenix, of course. And this is Harper.' She nods at a willowy Indian girl wearing an orange dress in a similar cut and fabric to mine.

'Welcome,' Harper repeats, giving me a smile this time.

'And Audrey,' Melody says, indicating a slender girl with mousy hair — the one I never got to meet in hospital — 'and Callum.'

Callum is sitting next to Audrey on a purple couch. Like Phoenix, he is wearing black trousers and a fitted t-shirt, but he is at least a head shorter, with curly blond hair. When I wonder how old he is, I receive an almost instant reply: he's fifteen. Should I block my thought-stream? But why? It's not as if I have anything to hide from my fellow captors.

Melody pats a green armchair next to a shiny green fridge. 'Have a seat, Violet. I'll leave you to it, shall I?'

No one replies, at least not aloud.

Don't say anything you don't want them to hear, Phoenix think-says, after the automatic doors slide shut behind Melody.

Yeah, I figured that. Swinging my eyes around the ceilings, I spot a tiny black object in the corner opposite the door. Camera, check. As if I expect anything less.

'So what happens in here?' I ask, taking note of the giant

e-screen on the wall. 'Do you watch movies? Play board games?'

Harper, who looks around my age, moves to the window. 'We do what they want us to do.' She places her palm on the glass. 'Puzzles. VirtReal simulations. Fitness training.'

'That sounds familiar,' I say, disappointed they haven't yet told me anything I don't already know.

'They're trying to make a vaccine,' Audrey says. 'They need our blood to try and work out how come we're still alive.'

That's not the only reason why they want our blood, Callum think-says. *They want to work out how we do this . . . right?*

You can't tell that from someone's blood. Audrey sounds so confident when she says that.

I guess that's why they keep scanning our brains. I glance towards the window, where Harper is still standing with her hand on the glass, a hot glow at the base of her spine. *Is your back sore?* I ask, and her colour flares scarlet. Oh no, I didn't mean to alert everyone else to her period cramps.

Wait. Phoenix's curiosity is yellow-orange. *You can feel Harper's cramps?*

Can we talk about something else? Harper is snappish.

Yeah, let's. I glance at the microphone/camera on the ceiling. *Why else do you think we're here? If it's just about vaccines, they could have got all they needed off us without bringing us all the way out here.*

Audrey just looks at me, scratching the underside of her arm. My implant doesn't feel itchy anymore, but remembering it's still there makes me feel invaded all over again.

Phoenix think-says, *It's obvious, isn't it? What's the most obvious use for a bunch of teenagers with the ability to read other people's minds?*

Espionage. Callum cracks his knuckles. There's another sound echoing around the building too, a whump-whump that's setting up vibrations in my bones, but I'm too distracted to try and figure out what it is.

What, they want us to be spies? Harper's upper lip curls. Audrey hugs herself. The noise from outside is getting louder. Whump-whump. Whump-whump.

Either that, or they think we're a threat. I stare directly into the camera. 'Do you think we're a threat?' I say, aloud this time.

Violet, ssh, Audrey think-hisses.

'Undoubtedly we're a threat.' Phoenix gives me an odd smile before strolling to the window. 'Well, look who's come to join the party.'

I don't need to look out of the window to see what Phoenix is seeing. No, I'm receiving Phoenix's thought-images loud and clear.

There's a man stepping out of a helicopter, the same man who told me not to be afraid a week ago, right before he took me hostage.

Let me introduce myself. My name is Doctor Noel Marlow, and I'm a neurologist.

I am not afraid, I think.

And yet, I am.

TWENTY-NINE:

ETHAN

O n Wednesday, I don't get out of bed until after ten am. Not because I'm asleep, but because I'm trying to contact Rawiri again. Soon after I strayed into our game, seconds after Rawiri spoke to me, everything went blurry and, damn it, I was sitting on an exercycle, captive in my body once more.

I don't think I made that up. I spoke to him, I did.

Didn't I?

'How was that?' Bruno had asked.

'Boring,' I'd said and stormed off to my stupid room.

Now it's five past ten, and I'm standing in the shower, my eyes closed. Trying to make contact with Violet. Failing to make contact with Violet.

Damn it, damn it. I wonder if I'll see Marlow today. I need to push him harder, find out what's really going on, work out how I'm going to get out of here.

'I want to see Doctor Marlow,' I say when Bruno brings a tray of food to my room.

Bruno deposits the tray on the desk. 'You can't.'

I scowl at him. 'Why not?'

Bruno passes a hand over his buzz cut. 'He's gone overseas. Conference.' Flitting through Bruno's thoughts, I find out that Marlow has gone to Australia. I can even hear Bruno's memory of Marlow's syrupy voice. *I'll be taking the private jet. Have you told Carol to book the helicraft for when I arrive?*

Private jet and helicraft? For a conference? As if.

'What sort of conference?' I ask, playing along.

'Neurology.' Bruno's lie is crimson, unstable. 'He'll return in a few days.' He gestures at the tray. 'Hope you like waffles.'

'They're OK,' I say, rifling through his mind as fast as I can before he leaves. The images from the other day are clearer this time. Five ambulances on a tarmac. Bruno helping load five stretchers onto a plane with no markings. Destination, Alice Springs.

Does that mean Violet has been taken to Australia, the others too? How did they get past Customs? Did they even use passports? And who, exactly, are *they*?

Bruno blinks at me. 'You OK? You look a bit . . .'

'I'm feeling a bit off today.' It's not a complete lie. My heart is thudding uncomfortably.

Violet is in the middle of the desert, and I need to find her, need to get help.

But first, I need to get out of here.

After breakfast, Bruno takes me to a gym. I'm not entirely opposed to some exercise, especially since I seem to have been spending most of the last few weeks lying in bed or sitting on my butt. Also, for some reason, it's easier to *travel* when my body is in motion. Don't ask me how that works.

Before I start, Bruno asks me to remove my shirt so he can attach sticky dots to my chest.

'You're monitoring my heart rate? Don't these do that?' I grip the handlebars on the rowing machine.

'Yes, but we want to monitor the rhythm too.' He attaches a series of ECG dots next, and clips a small box onto the waistband of my Foundation-issue shorts. Presumably the doctors will be able to tell something from the peaks and wiggles on the read-out, which is like a foreign language to me, even after all my time in hospital.

I wonder, briefly, why they're not interested in my brain as well, before glancing around the room and noticing the now-familiar cigar-shaped boxes attached to the walls. Each one has a tiny blue light blinking in the bottom right corner. Accessing Bruno again confirms my suspicions — they *are* interested in my brain. Very, very interested, in fact. Turns out this whole room is a machine designed to pick up on my brain activity.

A WEB scanner, according to Bruno. Can they tell I'm accessing Bruno's thoughts right now?

Yet again, I wonder who *they* are, and how much they really know.

'. . . put this back on?' Bruno asks, and I realise I've zoned out again.

I take the t-shirt and tug it over my head. Grip the handlebars. Begin to row. The screen in front of me shows the prow of my boat skimming across the surface of a lake. A read-out along the bottom of the screen shows me my heart rate, my distance travelled, and my rate of travel.

I'm not interested in any of that, barely register Bruno leaving the room. No, my dream-flow is opening up and out, ripples in a giant pond. Swooping above the Foundation, over the forest, across the corrugated surface of the Waitematā Harbour. Over the roof tops, pausing briefly above my house — no one home — and a few streets over to a villa with a slate-grey roof and black weatherboards.

Rawiri is sitting in the upstairs bedroom. He's doing homework, for God's sake — why isn't he playing our game? *Rawiri*, I think-speak, but of course he can't hear me. I wait, knowing it's only a matter of time before he gets bored and starts playing with his first love. Meanwhile, I cast around, looking for someone, anyone who might be like me.

Nothing. Nothing. Nothing.

Some time later — I have no idea how much — I detect a shift in Rawiri's thought patterns, an orange glow. *Yes*, he's opening up our game. I move closer, feeling like an intruder crouching in my best friend's brain. If Rawiri's room were a NET scanner, they'd see something lighting up in his temporal lobes.

That would be me.

Rawiri twitches, and I retract slightly, worried I'm going to provoke a seizure or something worse. What if I cause him to have a stroke? Is that possible? How is any of this possible? A few days ago, I didn't even know what temporal lobes were.

Then he whispers, 'Time to get nasty,' and takes control of a stooped figure clad in black robes, a hood covering his raven-dark locks.

Ooh, I thought-whisper. It's Ariel, Keeper of Secrets and Master Healer. I created Ariel last summer, but the imagery is all Rawiri's. *When two minds are greater than the sum of their parts*, I think, and am momentarily distracted by — what? Ignoring the uncomfortable sensation coming from I-don't-know-where, I watch Ariel step to the entrance of his cave to greet Roman, who is approaching on horseback.

Aware I don't have time to waste, I focus on Roman until I feel the horse moving between my thighs, and feel the glare of twin Death Stars beating on my shoulders.

'Greetings, Roman,' Ariel says. Around his neck is a vial containing the blood of his great-great-great-grandmother, the secret to his longevity. If the vial is lost, so is Ariel, along with his healing powers.

At least, I think that's how it's going to go, but I was still working out the final details when I got sick.

'Hey,' I say. Not very warrior-like, I know, but I need to get Rawiri's attention somehow.

'Did you program that in as a joke, Wright?' Rawiri mutters, his fingers flying over the keyboard.

Ariel says, 'The plague is spreading like wildfire, and the Meth Heads are rioting in the south. What news have you of the Dragon Queen?'

'The Dragon Queen needs your help,' I say.

'Roman, son of Agaron, no help can be given without sacrifice.' Rawiri selects an icon at the bottom of the screen and a fire springs up in front of me, causing my horse to rear up on his hind legs.

'Listen,' I say, after retreating a safe distance away, 'Roman's true father is being held hostage in a facility not far from here.'

Rawiri, frowning, types some more. Ariel says, 'Where? A castle? A dungeon?'

'Look,' I say, giving up on the double-speak. 'My father's name is Ethan, and he's being held against his will about ten kilometres southwest of Piha, in a building called the Foundation.'

Rawiri's thoughts go a bit haywire after that, a cacophony of purple and red and green, so loud I worry he really is going to have a seizure or something.

'Oh my God,' he says. 'Oh my God, oh my God.' He bends to start typing again, and I know what's he going to write before Ariel's mouth opens, something along the lines of, *Jesus, Ethan, do you need me to call the cops*, but I don't get a chance to hear Ariel's voice in his gravelly tones because at that moment I'm—

Writhing on the floor of the gymnasium, gasping for air. Four faces, two of which are female, crowd into my field of vision.

'Return to sinus rhythm,' one of the women says. I press my palm to my chest. It feels as though I've been hit by a cricket ball or kicked really hard. I wouldn't be surprised if something's broken.

Bruno crouches beside me, his fingers on the pulse at my neck, and I become aware of my heartbeat, wild and heavy.

'Defibrillation successful,' he says.

'What?' I rasp.

'We just shocked your heart back into normal rhythm,' one of the women says. 'You're lucky we were so close by.'

That's how I learn I've just survived a cardiac arrest.

THIRTY

VIOLET

Marlow isn't alone. When he enters the common room, a few minutes after the helicraft blades stop turning, he's accompanied by Melody and a middle-aged man in a black suit.

'I think you all know Doctor Marlow,' Melody says.

What do you think would happen if I deck him? Phoenix think-asks, in his usual sardonic tone.

I think those big guys would sedate you and haul you off somewhere, I think-reply, noting the bodyguards in the corridor. Five of them versus five of us. I bet I know who'd come off better in a fight.

I wouldn't be so sure about that, Phoenix think-says.

Marlow sits on the couch nearest to the door. Black Suit sits next to him, while Melody stays where she is, flanked by Thug One and Thug Two.

'Let me introduce you to Hans Bauer,' Doctor Marlow says. 'Chief of Intelligence at the ITA.'

Told you, Callum says. *Es-pio-nage.*

Audrey lets out a small noise and curls further into the couch, as if she wants to disappear. I know that feeling.

'ITA?' Phoenix says. 'Never heard of that before.'

'It's not something that is widely advertised,' Bauer says. He has a faint accent, which I'm guessing is German, if his name is anything to go by. I can't read his mind any better than I can read those of Marlow and his companions, and wonder, not for the first time, how they manage to block us.

Marlow, who is looking as crisp as ever in his bone-white suit and ice-blue shirt, says, 'Let me ask you, what is the biggest threat to our society today?'

'Infectious diseases,' Audrey says, at the same time as Callum says 'Terrorism.'

Marlow inclines his head. 'Actually, you're both correct.' He points his PA at the screen on the wall and it lights up. A camera pans over a group of women, men and children lying on mattresses in what looks like a very basic hospital. A man with an English accent announces, 'There have been four thousand deaths from a new strain of Ebola in the Congo since January.' The image on the screen changes, and we see a picture of a leg with an open wound oozing with pus. 'This patient lost both his legs and then his life due to an infection with a resistant strain of *Staphylococcus*. This strain, for the first time in history, is resistant to all known antibiotics,' the English voice says. 'Doctors fear that this will only be the first of many cases if a new antibiotic is not made available within the next year.' The next image is of children in a more modern hospital, their skin covered in the characteristic M-fever rash, their eyes red and inflamed. 'Meanwhile, despite modern medicine,' the voice continues, 'the M-fever death toll in Australia, New Zealand and Germany also continues to rise, with three hundred deaths registered in New Zealand since the first of January.'

144

'*Three hundred?*' Harper blurts, her shock reverberating within me.

'It's accelerating,' Melody says softly. 'If we can't develop a vaccine soon, this could turn into a pandemic that will make COVID-19 look like the common cold.'

'We desperately need a vaccine,' Marlow says. 'And yet, the one we'd pinned our hopes on hasn't performed to our expectations. Not only that, but our attempts to develop a more potent vaccine are being thwarted by the Holistics, who claim we are trying to poison people with medicines that they say do more harm than good. Some of them are targeting our scientists and doctors. Some may even be training as scientists and doctors themselves to sabotage the cause from the inside.'

I frown. 'In what way?'

Bauer says, 'Last week, a bomb was set off in a research facility in Boston, killing three scientists and injuring five more. Two days after that, a prominent pro-vaccination doctor was assaulted in a car park in Australia.'

'Are they OK?' Phoenix asks.

'They threw acid in her face.' Bauer takes his glasses off and polishes them with his jacket. 'She'll never see again.'

We all fall silent at that, until Harper says, 'So what has this got to do with us?'

Phoenix drums his fingers on his knee. 'Let me guess, it's something to do with the ITA, whatever that stands for.'

'The International Terrorism Agency.' Marlow nods at Bauer. 'Hans has a proposal for you.'

Frustration bubbles inside me. 'You make it sound as though we have a choice.'

Marlow gives me a half-shrug. 'I can't make you do anything you don't want to.'

He's full of it, Harper think-speaks.

Bauer crosses his legs. 'The International Terrorism Agency was set up five years ago in response to the global increase in terrorist attacks, of which I'm sure you're all aware.'

Of course I'm aware. Terrorism is a part of everyday life. I've grown up being taught to always be aware of the nearest exit in case I need to make a quick escape. Pity I didn't do the same when I was in hospital.

'And,' Bauer continues, 'I have reason to believe that you could help us. But of course, I don't believe everything I'm told. I wanted to see for myself.' He reaches up to his ear and removes a small hearing-aid-like object about the size of a button battery.

'Careful,' Marlow murmurs, touching his own ear. It makes me wonder what or whom they're listening to.

Bauer, ignoring him, focuses on Phoenix. 'Can you tell me what my mother's name is?'

'No,' Phoenix says. 'I can't.'

Audrey clears her throat. 'Ilsa Lea Bauer. Maiden name Lange.'

You idiot, Spelling, Harper think-says. Callum sighs and stares fixedly out of the window. Bauer's thought-stream tells me he's sceptical, that he's wondering if Marlow is tricking him somehow. I don't blame him.

'Very good,' Bauer says. 'And can you tell me what I ate for breakfast this morning?'

Audrey frowns. 'You're thinking the words bacon and eggs. But I'm—'

'Yes?' Bauer leans forward.

'That's not the images I'm getting from your memory. What you actually had was porridge with stewed rhubarb.'

Marlow smiles. Bauer murmurs, 'Lie detection, very good.' I catch his thought-stream for brief seconds, an orange flare of *stronger than Sarah* and *we've only just begun*, before he slots the device back into his ear and his mind becomes unreadable again.

Who the hell is Sarah? I think-ask, at the same time as Phoenix think-says, *So that's how they do it. I wonder what frequency those suckers are tuned into?*

Bauer takes control of the screen, using his PA to cast familiar, terrifying footage of the most infamous terrorist attack of the twenty-first century. A pair of planes flying into the Twin Towers, like something out of a bad dream, followed by blurred images of people jumping to their deaths to escape the burning, collapsing buildings. 2977 people dead, 6000 injured. Next are movie clips of the flowers placed as part of a memorial for the 2015 Paris attacks, then the more recent attacks in Rome, Barcelona and Melbourne.

The Melbourne attacks are still fresh in my mind from last year. I can barely stand to watch the footage of the smoke rising from the sports arena, where six terrorists detonated their bombs. Over 3000 dead, around 7000 injured. A new, horrifying record.

'It's very difficult to fight people who don't care about their own lives,' Bauer said. 'People who will die for their cause.'

'Even Holistics?' Phoenix has pushed the sleeves of his black top above his elbows. There are a series of small, circular scars on his right forearm I hadn't noticed before.

'We don't know yet.' Bauer straightens his cuffs. 'But we have reason to believe that a Holistic terrorist cell is planning a large-scale attack in Berlin. We have suspects, but we can't prove anything at this stage. We need kids — people — like you to help us.'

'So how come you had to bring us all the way out here to ask us that?' I gesture at the stark red world outside the window. 'Why have you imprisoned us?'

Marlow says, 'What you all have is very special. We need to help you learn to use it wisely, while reducing the chance of danger to yourselves and others.'

Callum squares his shoulders. 'Are you saying we'll be like some kind of special army?'

'For God's sake,' Harper mutters, while Audrey's eyes dart around us, like a frightened rabbit's.

'You'll be a Special Operations Unit operating under the direction of the ITA,' Bauer says. 'VORTEX.' The way he says it makes it sound as though the word is in capitals.

'VORTEX?' Phoenix rubs the scar on his arm.

'Virally Optimised Telepaths,' Marlow says.

'Virally Optimised?' Harper's eyes are blazing. 'You make it sound like we asked for this to happen to us.'

'Of course you didn't,' Marlow says evenly. 'But would you really want to give up these newfound abilities? It's not just the telepathy you've gained. Your processing speed is increasing rapidly — exponentially, one might say.'

'As measured by all those tests you keep giving us?' I ask.

'That's right,' Marlow answers. 'Did you think we were just playing games with you?'

'I'm not that stupid,' I snap.

'Of course not.' His voice is smooth. I feel like punching him.

It's not worth it, Phoenix think-says. I wish he'd stop being so sensible.

Bauer clears his throat. 'Of course, we would compensate you for your work. You'd be employees, with all accommodation and food provided, and anything else you desire. For a start, we'd like your help to flush out the Holistics, but as time goes on I hope you'll be willing to help us with other terrorists, too. You'll be given new identities, which may need to be changed from time to time.'

'New identities?' Audrey squeaks.

Oh come on, what did you expect? Callum think-says. His disdain is green, but beneath that I sense the golden glow of his excitement.

'Where will we live?' I ask.

'You'll stay here until you finish your training,' Marlow says. 'And after that . . . well, you'll go wherever you're needed.'

'As in, anywhere in the world?' Callum asks.

'Anywhere in the world,' Bauer confirms.

Awesome, Callum think-says.

Harper's thought-stream is less enthusiastic. *Who's to say they won't just get rid of us once they get the information they need?* she think-says.

Exactly, I think-reply. I don't trust them, I just don't. And yet, a part of me wants to believe what they say. Perhaps it won't be so bad — exciting, even. If we succeed, we'll prevent the fanatics from standing in the way of an M-fever vaccine that will save thousands of lives. Perhaps they'll let us return home if we're successful. There's no reason we can't do that . . . is there? And if not, then how hard could it be to escape, anyway?

As for Phoenix, I can't tell what he's thinking, because he's blocking me, and presumably the others too. I guess I'll find out what he thinks of all this later. Maybe.

THIRTY-ONE:

ETHAN

f I thought I was a prisoner before, after my cardiac arrest things
have gotten even worse. Now I'm confined in a monitored bed.
A couple of metres from the foot of my bed is a rectangular
box surrounded by glass, a box I think of as mission control, but
which my nurse calls the ward station. It's hardly a ward when
there are only two beds in here, and the other bed is unoccupied,
but whatever. Apart from that, it's like the intensive care unit all
over again, but this time the doctor is especially interested in my
heart.

It's not Doctor Marlow, who, presumably, is still at his so-
called conference in Australia. No, this doctor is a woman with
cropped silver hair and a tiny diamond stud in her nose. She
tells me her name is Jane Griffin, and that she's a cardiologist.
She tells me I can't get out of bed until they monitor my heart
for at least twenty-four hours, to see if there's any sign of the
arrhythmia that nearly killed me this morning.

I should be worried about that — and deep down, I am —
but my focus is on getting out of here and finding Violet, as
impossible as that seems. Still, I'll play along for now.

'I'd also like to do an echocardiogram, or ECHO,' she says.

'How's that different from an ECG?' I finger the dots on my chest, which are transmitting signals to the monitor above my bed.

'It's a specialised ultrasound of the heart, so we can see if your heart muscle has been weakened by the M-fever virus.' The cardiologist wheels a machine over to my bed.

'And what will you do if you find that?'

'It depends.' Griffin squirts gel onto my chest and begins to run the probe over my skin. 'Perhaps medication, perhaps an ICD.'

'A what?'

'An implantable cardioverter defibrillator. It will deliver a shock if you have an abnormal rhythm, just like they did this morning. But if the heart muscle is significantly weakened, well . . .'

'Well, what?'

'Let's not get ahead of ourselves,' Griffin mutters, squinting at the screen to her right. 'Here's your left ventricle, see? That's the chamber of the heart that pumps blood to the rest of your body.'

'Does it look OK?'

'Hmm. Well, it doesn't look quite as strong as I'd expect for a seventeen-year-old.' When I check to see if she's lying, I realise it's more a case of her downplaying the truth.

My heart is not great. In fact, the muscle strength is only thirty percent of what it should be at my age, because the M-fever has caused what Griffin calls a *severe cardiomyopathy*. I guess I should be panicking, but it's not as if I can do anything about that. No, I need to concentrate on what I *can* do, such as communicating with others outside of this building.

I wonder what Rawiri is doing, wonder if he's gone to the police after what I told him. Surely they must be looking for me, unless they've been given a reason not to? I wonder how wide the Foundation's reach is, whether they are controlled by or separate from the government. I try to reach out for Violet again. I'm expecting nothing, a blank, but to my surprise I'm tuning into . . . something. It's faint and blurry, but it's there.

Violet, I think-say. *Violet, can you hear me?*

There's no answer, but I think it's her. I think it is, because I can hear her heartbeat now, slow and steady.

'Huh,' Griffin says, startling me.

'What?' I ask.

Frowning, Griffin fiddles with the dials on the machine. 'I could have sworn . . . hmm.'

'Sworn what?' When she doesn't reply, I tune into her thought-stream again. Griffin is thinking, *inexplicable rise in ejection fraction*. She's thinking, *doesn't make sense*. She's thinking, *must have been mistaken*.

That's when I know Violet is definitely in my range, her heart beating in synchrony with mine. No, not just that. Somehow, her heart is augmenting mine, doing the work of two.

'Is it looking better now?' I ask, knowing already what the answer will be.

'Why, yes,' the cardiologist says, her brow furrowed. 'I guess I didn't have the right window before.'

That's what she's telling herself, because nothing else makes sense. Not to her, anyway.

That evening, I lie awake for hours after lights-out. The ECG tracing on the monitor above my head is steady, regular, reliable:

none of the runs of peaks I saw earlier today. Violet's heart, aiding and abetting mine. I can't even begin to imagine how that can be possible, like most of the things that have happened to me recently.

Violet, I think-send, over and over. *Are you there?*

I'm about to give up when I feel something new. A thrum, a whisper. *Ethan, is that you?*

My heart leaps, literally, because the monitor starts alarming. Crap. Seconds later, the night nurse appears beside my bed.

'Are you all right?' She presses a button on the monitor, silencing the alarm.

'Never been better,' I say. My heart rate slows. The nurse stares at the tracing for a moment before walking away.

Are you all right? Violet think-asks.

I am now you're here.

What happened?

I show her the events of this morning — what I can remember, anyway. *Oh my God*, Violet says. *Oh my God. Can they fix it?*

I think you already have, I think-say.

You don't know that for sure.

I think I do. I tell her about the echocardiogram, and how confused the cardiologist was when my weakened heart muscle began contracting normally again. *Right at the moment when I made contact with you.*

Oh. Wow.

What's been happening with you? I think-ask, so she tells me. The ITA. The Holistic Terrorists. VORTEX. Special training. I feel a strange jab of jealousy when she tells me about VORTEX. How come the Foundation don't want me to be part of that? Is it because they think I'm weak?

I spoke to Rawiri, I think-say, not wanting Violet to pick up on my stupid envy. *When he was playing Eternity. I told him where I was.*

Where did you tell him you were?

Out west. At the Foundation. What else should I have said?

But Ethan, she says. *You're not there, not anymore.*

What do you mean?

You've been transferred, she says. *You must have been.*

What? I don't remember that.

Neither did I, she think-says. *None of us do.*

But . . . what day is it?

Friday, Violet replies, and I realise I've lost two days. They must have sedated me again. I want to scream. I want to rip the implant out of my arm. And yet — and yet —

Where are you? I ask. *Are you close?*

Very close, she confirms. *We all are. Listen.*

And now I hear them, can feel their heartbeats, too. They're not as loud as Violet, not as strong, but they're there all the same. The collective.

Ethan, Violet think-says, *welcome to the Red Centre.*

THIRTY-TWO

VIOLET

On Saturday morning, we're allowed outside for the first time since we arrived. That is, it's the first time our bodies have been outside. We've all been travelling in our spare time, adopting whatever animals take our fancy. Phoenix is always a wedge-tailed eagle. I prefer to be an albatross. Harper usually travels as an owl. Callum is a hawk, and Audrey likes to be a godwit.

A godwit? I ask her. *Why a godwit?*

Godwits are amazing, she says. *They fly non-stop all the way from the Arctic to New Zealand every summer. Nine days, eleven thousand kilometres.*

She's right, that *is* pretty amazing. I wonder if my dream-flow will ever be capable of such feats. Somehow I doubt it.

Today, though, is the first time I've ever felt the heat of Central Australia on my human skin. It's early morning, nine am, but it's already twenty-eight degrees Celsius. Dash, our shooting instructor, tells us we're still eleven degrees below the day's maximum predicted temperature.

Like the others, I'm wearing earmuffs and safety goggles, a

tight-fitting t-shirt, lightweight trousers, boots. My feet are hot, but no one wears open-toed shoes out here, not when there are snakes and spiders and who-knows-what-else waiting to bite you.

The snakes aren't going to run after you, Phoenix had said, soon after we'd first exited the building. *Just try not to piss them off.*

At the moment, I'm trying not to piss Dash off. I can't help that my attention is wandering. All I can think about is meeting up with Ethan. I haven't seen Melody today, but as soon as I do, I'll ask her if I can visit him.

Dash's voice transmits through my earmuffs. 'Violet, this is not a game. If you can't focus, then I'm going to have to ask you to leave the firing range.'

'I'm focusing,' I mumble.

'Well, come on, where's that stance I taught you? And that's not how you hold it — were you even listening?' He rearranges my hands on the gun. 'And remember, keep your finger outside of the guard until you're ready to fire.'

'OK.' I hear a shot nearby, and almost simultaneously the clay bird on the metal track in front of us explodes. Phoenix doesn't need to be reminded how to fire a gun, any more than I need to be reminded that Ethan is within my immediate vicinity, his blood surging every time my heart contracts. It's something I'm vaguely aware of most of the time, but every now and then I feel an extra-hard thud in my chest, as if my heart is working overtime. Which, in effect, it is.

Can they fix it?

I think you already have.

Can that really be true? Am I really Ethan's lifeline?

'That's it.' Dash taps me on the elbow. 'Give that to me.'

Sighing, I give him the gun. He jabs his thumb towards the door behind us. 'Inside. You're a danger to everyone here.'

'It's not real,' I tell him. The VirtReal sim is as close as the Foundation staff are letting us get to firearms at the moment. I guess they don't trust us any more than we trust them.

Dash glares at me. 'Inside.'

Flushing, I scuttle inside the building. Melody emerges from a room to my left and mouths something at me.

I flip the earmuffs off so they're hanging around my neck. 'What did you say?'

'I said, are you OK?'

'I want to see Ethan,' I say, shivering a little as the air con flows over my skin.

Melody doesn't even look surprised. 'He's been sick. But I guess you already know that.'

'He's not sick anymore.' I lock eyes with her. She doesn't look away.

'He appears to be stable this morning.' She takes the earmuffs and goggles from me. 'All right,' she says, her expression softening. 'But just for a few minutes.'

'Why only a few minutes?'

'As I said, he's been sick. We don't want him to get over-stimulated.'

'He won't,' I say.

I guess we both know that's a lie.

Melody takes me to a lift bank halfway down the corridor. After descending to a floor labelled Two Below, she leads me through a series of locked doors with retinal ID, right into what feels like the centre of the spiral building.

'You've got ten minutes,' she says as the last set of doors open. I'm barely listening, too focused on the hospital-like surroundings in front of me. There are two beds, only one of which is occupied. Ethan is sitting up, and if it weren't for the ECG dots on his chest and the IV cannula in the back of his hand, I wouldn't have thought he was sick at all.

I step closer. 'Hey,' I say, aware that Melody is hovering right behind me.

'Hey.' Ethan pushes his hair out of his eyes. It's longer than when I last saw him, almost halfway down his neck. *Is she going to leave us alone?* he think-asks.

I turn. 'Can we have some time to ourselves?'

Melody hesitates. 'Sure.'

'It's not as if they're not listening in anyway,' I mutter, glancing towards the stern-faced nurse sitting in the office behind us. At least, I think she's a nurse.

'Yeah, no kidding.' Ethan clasps my wrist. I sit beside him, a complication of emotions whirling through me.

'You look OK.' Better than OK. He's got colour in his cheeks, and he looks more toned than when I last saw him — his chest broader, his arm muscles more defined.

'Did you think I wouldn't?'

'I wasn't sure.' I touch the spot between his eyebrows, and my heart, *our* heart, speeds up.

'Careful,' he murmurs before leaning forward to kiss me.

I draw in a shaky breath. 'I didn't know if I was ever going to see you again.'

'Ditto. What have you been doing?'

'I just came off the firing range.'

'Whoa.'

'Yeah, I was pretty useless. And yesterday we basically did boot camp.' Every muscle in my body is aching from the sprints, sit-ups, press-ups and jumping jacks. It was kind of fun, though. I switch to think-speak. *If nothing else, I'm going to be super-fit by the time I get out of here.*

I'm jealous. You look good. Like, better than when I last saw you.

You too. When he goes to kiss me again, I think-add, *Um, Melody doesn't want me to overstimulate you.*

Overstimulate me? He grins. *What did she think we were going to do?*

Stop, I think-say, embarrassed. *When are they going to let you out of here?*

Tomorrow, if my heart behaves.

Guess I'd better not overstimulate you then.

'Too late,' he whispers and kisses me slowly, his hand on my hip. *They're going to give me a room next to the rest of you, as long as I don't try and die again.*

Suppressing a shudder, I think-say, *They told you that?*

No, but that's what I got off Melody this morning.

Wait. I draw away. *You accessed her? But how did you get past her earpiece thing?*

Ethan shrugs. *I've kind of worked out how to bypass them. Sometimes, anyway.*

Wow. Did you find out anything else?

Only that they thought my heart was seriously screwed, but now they're not so sure. He touches the ECG dots. *I'm going to have to keep these on for a few more days, just in case.*

Well. They kind of suit you.

Yeah, really sexy. He laughs. Me, I feel hot all over. I've never been very good at this flirting business, especially with someone

I really like. But it doesn't matter, because Ethan is kissing me again and I almost forget where I am, at least until we are rudely interrupted.

'I'll have to ask you not to do that,' the nurse says from the foot of the bed.

Ethan scowls at her. 'What? Why?'

'We don't want you picking up an infection.' I feel a whoosh of air behind me: Melody entering again.

'Time to go, Violet,' she says.

Growling beneath my breath, I rise to my feet, my eyes on Ethan. *I'll talk to you later.*

He lifts his chin. *Later.*

You should come out with us, I think-say, as Melody escorts me out. *Tonight.*

Tonight? Where?

Outside. At night, we travel. You'll like it, I promise.

I like the sound of that.

'Dash is going to give you another chance,' Melody says. 'You need to concentrate this time, OK?'

'Sure,' I say, before sending one more message to Ethan. *Maybe tomorrow night, if you're in your own room, we can be alone . . . really alone.*

I love the sound of that, he replies, and I begin to feel hot all over again, even before we exit the building.

'Are you ready?' Dash asks a couple of minutes later, once I'm standing with my legs slightly bent, my hands clasped around the gun.

'Ready.' Aim. Fire. The clay pigeon shatters, and I feel an unexpected surge of satisfaction.

'Not bad,' Dash says. 'Not bad at all.'

THIRTY-THREE:

ETHAN

That night, after lights-out, I tune into Violet and the rest of the collective. If I had to describe to an outsider how I distinguish between them, I suppose I would say that each individual has their own colour, their own shape — and yet, there are no words for what it's really like. But I would try.

I would say that Harper is aubergine and circular, so perhaps it makes sense that she assumes an owl form for our travels. Audrey's essence is bark-coloured, slightly spiky but solid and earthy too. As for Phoenix, I don't know about him. His colour keeps shifting, blue-grey, and he has a habit of shutting himself off at unexpected moments, like a dropped PA call.

Travelling with the others is exhilarating, though. My dream-flow assumes the form of an Andean condor, my wingspan greater than any of the others. It's exciting and sad at the same time, knowing I can assume the form of a species that may well be extinct before the decade is over. Together, we swoop above the desert, through gorges, over the gigantic domed rocks that form Kata Tjuta. I see kangaroos and wallabies jumping, thorny devils scuttling beneath rocks, camels roaming in pairs. I hear dingoes yelping, a joey crying for its mother. I feel our collective heartbeat: slow, strong, steady.

Oh, wow, I say, as we approach the largest rock I've ever seen. *Is that—*

Uluru, Violet confirms.

Uluru is even more awe-inspiring than in the photographs. As we pass over it, I get a weird sensation, as if I've flown over some kind of giant magnet.

Do you think there's something under there? I ask, gazing across the deeply ridged surface.

Like what? Audrey asks.

I don't know. Bones?

Fossils, maybe. Phoenix's flight path curves, as if he's a plane circling an airport. *Although the rock started forming six hundred million years ago, so maybe not.* Meanwhile, Callum is dive-bombing a small animal, although I'm not sure why he's bothering. It's not as if he has a physical presence.

They run anyway, Callum replies. *They can sense us.*

You like being a predator, don't you? Harper's owl eyes are solemn, unblinking.

Better than being the prey, Callum says.

Do you trust him? I ask Violet, later, once we've returned to our bodies.

Of course, she says. *Don't you?* She knows I'm talking about Phoenix. So much of our communication is non-verbal now, something else that would be too difficult to explain to a normal person.

He's very . . . private.

He lost his whole family, Violet says. *He's a good guy once you get to know him.*

I'm sure.

Now who's being private? She's right, of course. I've blocked her, ever so briefly, in the hope she won't sense my flickers of jealousy. Best to change the subject, I figure.

I wish I could visit you. I gaze at the monitor above my bed. The ECG tracing is steady, regular.

They'll let you out tomorrow, she says. *Won't they?*

I hope so. Do you think I'll be able to come to your room? I want to kiss her. I want to hold her. I want to tell her — no, block, block, I don't want her to know *that* yet. Or rather, I'd like her to know but I'm too embarrassed to say it.

There you go again, she teases after encountering my temporary wall of silence, before adding, *The corridors are monitored, cameras everywhere. I haven't been able to find one in my new room yet, but I bet it's there somewhere. But maybe we can find a way.*

I hope so. Her colour has faded slightly, lemon rather than daffodil-yellow. Even virally optimised beings need their sleep.

I heard that.

I smile. *Sleep well, Vi. I'll see you tomorrow, I mean today.* When I check the monitor beside my bed, I see it's three am. The witching hour, my mother would say.

See you in the morning, Violet replies and then she's gone, but not gone, her heartbeat lulling me to sleep.

The next day, after a repeat echocardiogram and scrutinisation of my ECG readings, Griffin clears me for discharge. A woman called Melody arrives to take me to my new room. It feels good to stretch my legs again, to be released from my virtual chains.

Melody points out the others' rooms as we walk past. Mine is on the end, next to Callum's, whilst Violet's is farthest away and at the exact opposite end of the corridor. Funny, that.

'Where is V— the others?' I ask.

'They're with the hairdresser,' Melody says.

'The hairdresser?'

'That's right. I'll come and get you in half an hour or so, OK?' She nudges a door to my left. 'There's your bathroom.' Is that her way of telling me I stink? She's probably right, since I haven't had a proper wash since I left New Zealand. Thinking of that gives me a horrid, empty, melancholic feeling. Does my family think I'm dead? What if I never see them again?

The memory of Violet's voice echoes in my mind. *He lost his whole family.*

Yeah, Violet, and so have we, haven't you figured that out yet?

I stay in the shower for a long time, taking a ridiculous pleasure in the apple-scented shampoo and conditioner, the frangipani soap, the water pounding my body. I'm tempted to remove the ECG dots, but don't want to invite a team of staff brandishing defibrillator paddles.

I'm towel-drying my soon-to-be-cropped hair, wearing only a pair of trousers, when there's a rap on the door.

'Hey.' It's a muscular guy with very short blond hair and Asian characters tattooed above his left eyebrow. He leans on the door frame. 'You must be Ethan. I'm Phoenix.'

'I figured.' I dump the towel on my bed. 'You look kind of different when you're not being an eagle.'

'Yeah, I reckon I make a better bird than a person.' He straightens up. 'I've come to fetch you for the communal haircut and iris tattoo. Pick a colour.'

I grab a t-shirt and accompany him down the corridor. 'They tattooed your *eyes*?'

'It didn't hurt once they put the anaesthetic drops in,' he says, and I notice his eyes are slightly bloodshot, his irises steely grey. Like me, he's wearing black combat trousers and a tight-fitting black t-shirt with a spiral emblem over the left breast.

'Is Phoenix your real name?'

His brow furrows. 'Yeah.' I want to ask him to translate his tattoo, but feel stupid, so I don't. He stops next to a lift and presses a button. 'How are you feeling?'

'I'm good. Now.'

Phoenix nods, his eyes on the display above the lift entrance, which says Two Below. 'Lucky for Violet, huh?'

'You know about that?' I watch the read-out change to *One Below*, then *Ground*.

She told me, he says, slipping into think-speak as we step inside the lift. When I don't reply, he think-adds, *So, I'm not sure how close you guys need to be to each other for that to keep working.*

The doors shut. I think-say, *I have no idea either. I don't even know how it works.*

Well, he says, *you might want to take a look at this.* He shows me a memory, a recent one, I'm guessing. In the memory, Violet is kneeling next to a couch on which a girl is lying face-down, her head in her arms. Violet's hand is on the girl's lower back.

Who's that? I think-ask.

Harper. She had bad cramps. Before.

Are you saying Violet is some kind of healer? The lift doors have opened.

I think so. Phoenix steers me out of the lift. I hear voices and laughter, Violet's among them. My heart, *our* heart, leaps.

Hey, Ethan, Violet think-says, before I've even set eyes on her, before Phoenix sends a message that only I can hear, one I need to block from Violet.

We need to protect her at all costs. Do you get it?

I'm not sure I do. How does the healer need protecting? I'm the one who nearly died, who could still die if Violet is taken out of my range. But I'm blocking *him* now, because we've just entered the dressing room or whatever the hell they call it, and Violet's cheeks are glowing and her newly blue eyes are sparkling and her freshly dyed hair is flowing over her shoulders in strawberry-blonde waves.

Do you like it? she think-asks, spinning around in her chair. I want to tell her I don't care how she looks, that hearing her blood sing in my ears is enough, but I block that and think-tell her, *You look great*. The others step forward to introduce themselves. *Welcome*, they think-say. *Welcome, welcome*.

I sit in a chair. Choose blue-black hair dye, moss-green for my iris tattoo, a sterling-silver hoop to go through my left eyebrow.

I'm with my people. I'm with my Violet. My homesickness lifts. My jealousy melts away. I am healed, and I am strong, and I am going to free us all if it's the last thing I do.

THIRTY-FOUR

VIOLET

Over the next four weeks, we assume a routine. As much as I resent being kept prisoner, I'm enjoying hanging out with the other members of the collective, or VORTEX. I guess we understand each other in a way no one else could. Much of our telepathy is non-verbal, imparted through the colour of one another's emotions or images or other ways that can't be described. I don't mind the routine either, after several weeks during which I've had no idea what each day will bring.

We begin each morning with a communal breakfast. Our dining room has floor-to-ceiling windows overlooking the increasingly familiar stark, red landscape. The temperature inside is always a carefully controlled twenty degrees Celsius. Outside, the temperatures range anywhere from eleven to forty degrees.

After breakfast we always have physical training of some sort. One of my favourites is mixed martial arts, with Dash as our instructor. Despite his age, which must be early fifties, he's fitter than the rest of us. He tells us he participates in an ultra-marathon every year, running hundreds of kilometres through extreme environments such as the Sahara Desert and the Arctic

Circle. He also tells us that he used to be an undercover cop, but switched career paths eight years ago.

'Why did you give up?' Callum asks.

'You can only go undercover for so long. It changes you, in some ways for worse, in some ways for better.' Dash hesitates. 'You know what, though? You learn that it's quite rare for people to ever be purely good or purely evil.'

'It must be really hard,' Ethan says. 'Becoming friends with someone and then having to turn them in to the authorities.' We're sitting on the mats, warming down after a session where we've learned some basic chokes, throws and kicks.

Yeah, chokes. We're learning how to disable our opponents, or, if we have no choice, how to kill them. I'm disturbed by how little that is bothering me.

You do what you must to survive, I guess.

'I don't think I'll have trouble turning in a terrorist who wants to blow up babies,' Callum says.

'Me neither,' I agree, shuddering at the thought of all the innocent children killed in the recent attacks.

Our first session after lunch is foreign languages. As the days pass, we learn to converse in French and German. Next is Hebrew, Arabic and Farsi. In my other life, my old life, I had limped through basic French and had barely passed my Level 1 exam. But my new brain seems to absorb everything — from books and the memory banks of our teachers — as if by osmosis, building new networks at an exponential rate.

'Listen to this,' Audrey says one day. '*Whoever fights monsters should see to it in the process that he does not become a monster. And if you gaze long enough into an abyss, the abyss will gaze back into you.*'

'Still reading Nietzsche?' Phoenix asks. 'Sounds more

exciting than this.' He holds up the Torah, which is a Jewish holy text.

'Wasn't Nietzsche a Nazi?' I tuck my legs beneath me. We're sitting in the library, which is decked out with leather armchairs and tangerine-coloured rugs. There's even a fireplace, which none of us have lit yet.

Audrey frowns. 'No. I mean, the Nazis liked to quote him, but I think he could be interpreted in many ways. He died way before the Nazi Party was formed. What are you reading, Vi?'

'Guess.' I turn my book face-down, so no one can see what I've been reading. '*Even the darkest night will end and the sun will rise.*' I'm blocking them, so they can't access the answer straight from my thought-stream.

'Batman,' Callum says. Ethan laughs.

'Peasants,' I sniff.

Phoenix says, 'Victor Hugo, *Les Misérables*.' Once again, I wonder why someone so intellectual went into the army. His sardonic thought-voice slips into my meanderings. *Snob.* What the hell, how did he overcome my block so easily? When I try to reciprocate by accessing *him*, I come up against the usual wall.

Ethan reclines on the couch, his head at one end, his legs draped over the other. 'We should come up with our own quotes.'

'All for one and one for all?' Callum suggests.

Harper's upper lip curls. 'We're not Power Rangers.'

'That's from *The Three Musketeers*, actually,' Phoenix says. Of course. I glance at him, wondering, not for the first time, what the Japanese characters above his left eyebrow mean, and am surprised to get a thought-reply.

Johnno? I ask, as the others banter between themselves. *Who's Johnno?*

I'll tell you someday, he replies, and I pick up on a grey stream of emotion, pulling me in and down, before he blanks me out again. Blinking, I focus on the others. They're quoting Oscar Wilde, lyrics from their favourite songs, Winston Churchill.

'Together, we are infinite,' I say, and feel everyone's gaze on me.

'Together, we are infinite,' Audrey says slowly. 'I like that.'

'Alone, we are nothing,' Ethan adds, and something squeezes inside my chest, as if to remind me that my heart is doing the work of two.

'I don't know if I agree with that,' Phoenix says from his chair in the corner.

Ethan sits up. 'You wouldn't.'

'What do you mean?' Phoenix's tone is as flinty as his eyes.

'Well,' Ethan says, 'you're not really a team player, are you?'

A hush falls upon us. Even our thought-streams seem to be temporarily paralysed, as if we're waiting for something to happen.

'I've got a better motto,' Phoenix says after several long seconds. 'Don't trust anyone.' He gets to his feet and walks out, still holding the Torah.

'Well, I like it,' Audrey says after a short silence. *'Together, we are infinite. Alone, we are nothing.* Someone will be quoting *us* in fifty years' time.'

'Because we're famous, or infamous?' I ask.

'Both.' Callum stands up. 'I'm bored of this — is it time for water polo?'

We swim most days, in between languages and our second afternoon session, which usually consists of VirtReal exercises, such as navigating our way through foreign cities. The pool water is always a perfect aquamarine, just like the sky overhead, which is invariably clear and cloudless.

Today, I'm lounging around in the deep end with Ethan and Harper when I hear a voice say, 'Hey, guys.' It's Bruno, wearing bright yellow swimming trunks. He's accompanied by Dash, who is wearing black shorts and a grin. I like Dash. I'm not so sure about Bruno. He seems to think a lot of himself, maybe because he's quite good-looking, if you like the square-jawed type.

Bruno is one of the doctors. He's twenty-nine years old, as he often likes to tell us, which makes him the youngest member of staff.

'Mind if we join you?' Without waiting for an answer, Dash dives in and starts swimming with long, sure strokes.

Pretty good abs for an old guy, Ethan think-says.

It's not his abs I'm looking at, Harper think-replies, before calling out, 'Are you going to get in or just stand there looking pretty?'

Bruno's lips curve upward. 'I don't know, you might have to give me a lesson.'

Harper sits up on the side of the pool, her boobs almost falling out of her bikini top. 'In swimming or looking pretty?'

Bruno's gaze travels up and down her body, from her barely contained boobs to her g-string bikini bottoms. 'Both,' he says, before plunging in and powering towards the other end of the pool.

'Flirt,' Harper mutters, as if *she* can talk.

Puke. Ethan brushes his fingers past my thigh. *Want to come for a walk before the VirtReal session?*

'Sure,' I reply, looking across to the other side of the pool, where Phoenix is sitting in a deckchair, reading a book.

'I'll get our towels.' Ethan hoists himself out and strolls over to the bench. I climb up the steps on the side near the deckchairs, and hover in front of Phoenix.

'*Slaughterhouse-Five*,' I read off the cover. 'Looks really old.'

'Published in 1969.' He slides his sunglasses up on top of his head.

'What's it about?'

'It's satire. An anti-war novel, basically.' He's blocking me, as usual. 'Don't say it.'

'Say what?' I'm dripping on his thigh, but he doesn't seem to notice.

'What's an army grunt doing reading an anti-war novel?'

'I wasn't going to say that,' I reply, irritated that he's picked that out of my thought-stream. Glancing away, I see Harper throwing a ball at Bruno's head. He ducks, laughing, before hurling it at Ethan, who drops our towels to catch it.

I look back at Phoenix. 'Is it good?'

'Yeah. You should read it.' He swipes water off his thigh.

'Read me a line,' I say, a curious sensation rippling through me. It's as if Phoenix can see right into the centre of me, and it's . . . unsettling.

His tattooed irises — grey with blue flecks around the pupil — on mine, Phoenix says, '*And I asked myself about the present: how wide it was, how deep it was, how much was mine to keep.*'

'Mine to keep,' I repeat. At the moment, it feels as if nothing is mine to keep.

Nothing is mine to keep, Phoenix think-echoes, and an image flashes, unbidden, in my hindbrain. A white roof. Thick, unmoving air. The scent of blood and—

Phoenix's pupils dilate. He touches my wrist, *did you* . . . and then Ethan is behind me, wrapping a protective arm around my chest.

'Everything OK?' he asks. We're all three blocking each other, block-block-block, which is good, because I don't know what happened just then. A memory from Phoenix? Some kind of premonition?

Phoenix lowers his sunglasses over his eyes, picks his book up again.

'All good,' he says, his tone dismissive.

As we enter the climate-controlled interior of the building, Ethan says, 'What were you guys talking about?'

'Just his book,' I say, still blocking him. 'Nothing interesting.'

My favourite time to swim, though, is in the evening. I float for ages, gazing into the endless Milky Way. I'd never seen so many stars at once before I came out here. Could be I'm even falling in love with the outback, although I fear it, too — if I ever got lost out there, I know I'd be dead within hours.

And, then, there is Ethan.

He usually swims with me at those times, too. We wait until everyone else is out of the pool before we drift together, communicating without words. It's one of the few times we're alone. There are also more intimate times, when we sneak into each other's beds at night, although it's hard to imagine we're ever truly alone, that we're ever not being monitored.

Still, we push the boundaries as much as we can. We always draw the covers over our heads before taking over where we left off the night before. At first we're shy, kissing with our clothes on — Ethan in his boxer shorts, me in my t-shirt — but as each night passes, we become more adventurous. It's addictive, the feel of Ethan's bare skin against mine, his mouth on the most intimate parts of me. Our hearts speed up as we bring each other closer and closer to the edge, until I'm not sure if I'm strong enough to keep both our hearts beating.

Don't leave me, he whispers.

Don't leave me, I whisper back.

Together, we are infinite.

And we dare to think that *they* don't know, or don't care.

THIRTY-FIVE

ETHAN

One morning I wake up and realise it's the fifteenth of December, and my birthday. Today I am eighteen years old, and legally an adult. I could vote, if I were a free man.

But I'm not.

The Foundation kitchen staff make me a cake, and everyone sings 'Happy Birthday' over breakfast. It just makes me feel homesick. My family probably think I'm dead after all these weeks away. I'm old enough to vote, but who knows if I'll ever be able to do that? I'm being groomed for a role I never asked for.

Violet, sensing my mood, asks if I want to go for a walk at lunch time. After gobbling down our sushi, we slip out of the building. The midday heat is intense, the air thick, but for the first time since I got up, I feel as though I can take a deep breath.

We stroll towards a cluster of boulders on the northwest perimeter. The fence is only a few strides away, and is at least three metres high. If one of us tried to climb over it, we would get a shock — literally — but it's more to keep intruders out than us in. Even if one of us escaped, we'd be screwed without a vehicle. It's not the New Zealand bush. You can't just make a bivouac and drink stream water. Here, you could walk for a hundred kilometres, probably more, without coming across water or shelter.

A human being can survive six days at the most without water. I know, because I looked it up a couple of years ago, when I was learning about the human body in biology.

Once in the narrow oblong of shade cast by the ghost gum, Violet presses my body against the trunk. 'Happy birthday,' she says before kissing me to distraction.

'Do you think they'll miss us this afternoon?' I ask, once we've stopped to inhale. So much for being able to breathe.

'What are you suggesting?' Violet says, then laughs. *Oh. Right.*

Well, it is my birthday. I'm only half-joking. I know we can't have unprotected sex, even if it's only once. That's what the rational part of my brain says, anyway. The irrational part is saying, *Oh my God, I'm eighteen and still a virgin and if we weren't trapped here then we would be doing it by now, maybe right now.*

'I'm sure they could get hold of some birth control for us if we ask.' Violet's brow wrinkles. 'What? Why are you looking at me like that?'

'They'll say no,' I say, uncertainly.

'Why? If they want us to work for them, then surely they're interested in keeping us happy? It's not an unreasonable request.'

'You make it sound so easy,' I say, but I kiss her again, stroking her curves. 'Who will you ask? Melody?'

'Uh-huh.' Violet wipes sweat off her brow. 'As soon as she gets back.'

'Oh. Yeah.' Melody has gone to New Zealand for the week.

'Unless you want to ask Bruno for, you know, something else.'

As much as I don't want to wait another week — a whole week! — I just can't imagine asking Bruno for condoms. 'No,' I say. 'Besides, the pill is heaps safer, right?'

'Right. Or I could get one of those hormone injections.' She lets out a small noise, probably because now it's me pressing *her* against the trunk while I kiss her. We're so caught up in what we're doing, or nearly doing, that neither of us registers Bruno's presence until he's right behind us.

'You're late for class,' he says, his eyes flicking between Violet and me.

'We were just coming,' I lie.

'I'll walk with you,' he says, and he does, all the way to the library.

'Nice out there?' Harper asks when Violet and I sit on opposite couches, both of us ignoring Bruno.

'Hot as hell,' I say. Bruno huffs and leaves. I reach for the nearest book I can see, a Chinese textbook of mathematics, my equivalent of taking a cold shower.

And yet, I have something to look forward to. I think. I hope.

After dinner that evening, Phoenix asks if anyone wants to play basketball.

'Basketball?' Callum frowns. 'Where?'

Phoenix tips peanuts into his palm. 'There's a hoop outside. I saw some of the staff playing last night.' We're sitting in the common room, watching some rubbish zombie series. It makes me wonder what's happening with the M-fever epidemic at home, and if there are others like us. If so, where are they? Is that why Melody's gone back to New Zealand for the week?

'I'll come.' Callum jumps up.

'Yeah, me too,' I say, and Violet and Harper say they're in too. Audrey, who is curled up in a beanbag with a Russian romance, says she'll pass.

The sun has set already, so we play by the glow of the security light. It's still warm, twenty-five degrees at least, and I'm soaked with sweat after the first ten minutes. We've teamed up, Callum and the girls against Phoenix and me, and Phoenix and I are getting whipped.

'You didn't tell us you had a secret weapon,' I say after another fifteen minutes, by which time the score is thirty-five goals to ten.

Harper laughs, her teeth shiny pearls under the security light. 'Wait, did I forget to tell you I represented our school in basketball?'

'Hey, I thought I was the secret weapon,' Callum protests.

'Yeah, you're just here to look pretty,' Harper says, and Callum elbows her. Harper gives him a shove back and Callum stumbles, twisting before going down hard on his butt.

'Aargh,' he yells, clutching his leg.

'Oh no!' Harper rushes over to him. 'Are you OK?'

'No, I think I've broken my . . . Aargh!' He's pale, his eyes wide. Violet crouches beside him, but he bats her away. 'Don't touch it!'

'Settle down,' Phoenix says. 'Let her help you.' I sense, rather than feel, Violet's channelling of Callum's pain. Callum groans and lies back. He flinches when Violet touches his leg but doesn't move when she gently curls her fingers around his ankle.

'Is it broken?' I ask.

'Yeah.' She sits cross-legged beside him, still clasping his ankle. 'Is that any better?'

'It's not as bad as it was,' Callum mumbles.

Harper shuffles her feet. 'Shall I get Bruno?'

'*No*,' Phoenix and I chorus.

'I'll get you a drink of water then,' Harper says, and takes off.

I sink down beside Violet, the concrete warm on my thighs. 'How long do you think it will take?'

'I have no idea.' Her breathing is slightly rapid, whether from the exercise or the effort of the healing, I'm not sure. 'It still feels quite weak. I don't know how to explain it.'

Maybe we should move him inside, Phoenix think-says. *Away from prying eyes.*

And where would that *be?* I think-ask.

We'll manage, he replies, as cryptic as ever.

Several minutes later, we're in the common room. Violet and Callum are sitting on a couch with a throw draped over them, Callum's leg in Violet's lap.

You should be a doctor, Callum think-says.

I don't really like the sight of blood. Violet tips her head back, closes her eyes. It takes it out of her, I think, this healing business. I have no idea how she copes with my heart twenty-four-seven.

Remind me to have you handy if I decide to go rock-climbing, Harper says, before wandering out of the room.

Or end up in a terrorist attack, Audrey adds, and we all look at each other.

Violet's mouth twists. *I'm not sure my abilities extend to raising someone from the dead. Just saying.*

Imagine that. I gesture at the e-screen. *Virally optimised Zombies. We'd be lethal.*

Everyone laughs, even Callum, who is reverting to his usual puppy-like self.

Two hours later, Violet says he's fixed, good as new, and Callum immediately tests it out by jumping off the couch.

'Genius,' he says.

'Don't mention it.' Violet yawns.

'Are you sure it was broken?' Audrey asks.

'I'm sure.' Violet yawns and gets to her feet. 'I'm off to bed.'

'I'm turning in too,' I say, ignoring the knowing smirks of the others. It's not as if our relationship is secret. Seems nothing is around here.

We're halfway to our rooms when I hear someone say, 'Hey, guys,' and Harper slips out of a door to our left. 'How's Callum?'

'Fixed,' I say. 'Where've you been?'

'I was in the library.' Harper smooths her locks. 'Just needed a bit of quiet time.'

I glance over my shoulder just in time to see Bruno emerging from the same door, which is definitely not that of the library. He barely looks at us, just ducks his head and hurries in the opposite direction.

Were you in Bruno's room just now? Violet think-asks.

Are you kidding? Harper's thought-stream is tinged pink. *I mean, I was*, she think-adds, *but only for a minute. I asked him to look in my ear because it was a bit sore.* She tugs on her left earlobe. *Thought Violet had enough to do.*

Well, Violet think-says, *hope he had a good look.*

'It was nothing,' Harper mumbles, escaping down the corridor to her room.

'Notice how she was blocking us when she said that?' I murmur, taking Violet's hand.

'Hard not to,' Violet says, think-adding, *Maybe you should try and access Bruno, see what they really got up to.*

I haven't been so successful at that lately, I think-reply. *Think they've adjusted their blocking devices. Bastards.* We halt outside Violet's room, and I kiss her by the door. 'Have a good sleep.'

'Aren't you going to come in?'

'Thought you were tired.'

'I am. But I don't mind you being there while I fall asleep.' Violet tugs me inside and we strip down to our underwear before slipping beneath the covers, where she lies with her head on my chest.

You OK? I stroke her hair.

I'm fine. I just need a good sleep. She's drifting already, her thought-stream slowing. I breathe in, out, in, out, listening to the comforting rhythm of our heart.

I love you, Vi, I think-say, but she's already asleep.

THIRTY-SIX:

VIOLET

C hristmas is coming, and I have no idea what to give
Ethan.

No, I do have an idea, but I don't know if I'll be
able to give it to him straight away, or if I'll have to give him
some sort of voucher. *To be redeemed once we have our contraception
sorted.*

I never thought I'd be so happy to see Melody climbing out
of the helicraft. It's the twenty-second of December, three days
before Christmas. My good mood is only slightly soured by the
appearance of Marlow behind her, along with Bauer.

'Looks like we're about to have a meeting,' Ethan says. We've
just finished our martial arts session, and I'm hanging out for a
shower. So much for *that*. Bruno pokes his nose in the gym and
asks us to accompany him to the Octagon.

The Octagon is a room I've only been in once before,
when Dash took us on a guided tour of the Foundation. It's an
eight-sided room (yeah, no kidding) containing a circular table
surrounded by white leather seats.

'This is cool.' Callum sits on a chair and spins around.

Harper rolls her eyes at him. 'Don't go flying out of there or you'll be needing Violet again.'

'Baby, I need you,' Callum warbles.

'I love it when you speak dirty to me,' Ethan mutters, and Callum gets a fit of the giggles, but stops as soon as Bauer enters.

'Good morning.' Bauer sits at the head of the table, or at least, the side directly opposite the wall that doubles as a screen. Marlow sits to his right, the windows behind him, while Melody plants herself next to me.

'Hi, Violet,' she says, as if we're old friends.

'Hi,' I say, cautiously, because I've noticed how Bauer's gaze keeps returning to me. I swipe my hand over my mouth in case there are remnants of breakfast there, and avert my eyes.

'Good morning, Mr Bauer,' Ethan whispers in a robotic voice, as if he's five years old and addressing his primary school teacher. Maybe I should be adopting his strategy of turning everything into a joke. Maybe it will help get rid of this churning in my stomach.

'Something to share with us, Mr Wright?' Marlow asks. Ethan doesn't say anything, just slumps into his chair.

'I hear VORTEX is progressing well.' Bauer strokes his silver moustache, a new addition since we last saw him. 'You must all be looking forward to some . . . time away.'

Callum sits bolt upright. 'Time away? Are you going to send us on an assignment?'

'We would like to send two of you on an assignment.' Bauer's looking at me again. *Oh my God*, I think. *Oh my God*.

You're in, Ethan think-says, just before Bauer says, 'Violet, would you be willing to travel to Germany?' As if I have a choice.

'Sure,' I say, and then, quickly, 'Do I get to choose who

comes with me?' I reach beneath the table for Ethan's hand and give it a squeeze.

Bauer and Marlow exchange glances. Marlow says, 'Actually we think it'd be best if Phoenix accompanies you.'

'But he can't.' Anxiety rises up my throat. I don't look at Ethan, don't look at Phoenix either. I need to stay close to Ethan. If I don't, he might . . . he might . . .

Don't worry about me, Ethan think-says. His colour is dull green, as if he'd resigned himself to that fact even before Marlow announced it would be Phoenix, as if he already knew.

'I'm sure Phoenix is quite willing and able to go with you,' Marlow says. 'What do you say, Phoenix?'

Phoenix's eyes flicker. 'Sure.' *His* colour is granite, impenetrable.

I'm not going to give in that easily. 'I think Ethan should come with me. We'll work better as a team. We understand—'

Melody cuts across me. 'Violet, it's *precisely* because of your relationship with Ethan that we don't want him to go with you. You can't afford to be distracted.'

'But I—' Why isn't Ethan saying anything? Why is he dropping my hand like that? And how come he's blocking me too?

'If the rest of you don't mind leaving the room,' Bauer says softly, 'I would like to speak to Violet and Phoenix. Alone.'

When Bauer says he wants to talk to us alone, he means it. Even Marlow and Melody depart.

'You may wonder why I chose the two of you for the first mission,' Bauer says, once the door has closed behind Marlow.

I clench my fists, digging my knuckles into my thighs. 'Can I stay here?' I don't really want to stay — it could be my chance to escape — but I can't leave Ethan either. He could die without me.

You don't know that, Phoenix think-says.

It's not the kind of chance I want to take, I shoot back.

Bauer doesn't answer that, not directly. Instead, he takes a micro-PA out of his pocket and taps on it. The wall in front of him lights up.

'Ever been to Germany?' His tone is conversational, as if he hasn't cottoned on to the fact that I'm freaking out, big time.

'No,' Phoenix says. I press my lips together, shake my head.

Bauer gestures at the screen, where an electro-magnetic train with a dome-shaped nose is hurtling into a railway station. The sign on the wall says *Zoologischer Garten*.

'Do you know where this is?' he asks.

'The M-Bahn,' I say. 'The Berlin underground.' It featured in a German thriller I read the other night, although they were called U-Bahn in the old days, before the magnetic trains were invented.

'Zoo Station,' Phoenix murmurs. 'Just like the song.'

'Song?' I have no idea what he's talking about.

'Never mind.' Phoenix bends forward. 'So you're sending us to Berlin? When?'

'Tomorrow. I've booked you on the direct flight from Darwin to Frankfurt, and you'll connect to Berlin from there. Business class, of course. Bruno will accompany you and make sure you get to your accommodation safely. Your passports will be on your PAs and will match the facial recognition software and retinal ID that we have loaded onto the international customs database.'

Bauer taps on his micro-PA and the screen on the wall changes again. A transformed Violet stares back at me, with her strawberry-blonde hair and intense blue eyes. The name has changed, too. My new name is Liesl Meyer, and from the date of birth, I see I am already eighteen years old, eight months before my real birthday.

'Liesl Meyer.' Bauer taps his PA and the image changes again. 'And Wolf Schwarz. I recommend you start addressing each other by these names from today, so you get used to them.'

'Wolf Schwarz,' I echo, remembering that 'schwarz' means 'black' in German. *Wolf Black. Black Wolf.* A micro-shiver winds its way down my spine. Black was *my* name.

Bauer says, 'You are law students, although you are currently on holiday. You're boyfriend and girlfriend.'

'Boyfriend and girlfriend?' I squeak.

Phoenix rolls his eyes at me. I hunch into my chair.

'You're actors,' Bauer says smoothly. 'Have you ever been to the theatre?'

I give him a stiff nod. He inclines his head. 'Good. I want you to spend today familiarising yourself with the geography and culture of Berlin. Speak to each other in German, practise masking your New Zealand accents. As for your assignment . . .'

The image on the screen changes. 'This is the first individual we are interested in.' The guy on the screen is about early thirties, with sandy hair and white-framed glasses. 'Thomas Neumann is a microbiologist, and is married to,' the screen changes again, 'Klara Becker, a former physiotherapist but now full-time mother and caregiver to their eight-year-old daughter, Mia.'

The next photo shows the couple standing on either side of a girl who looks much younger than eight. She is sitting in a wheelchair, her head lolling to one side. Bauer says, 'Mia has been suffering from seizures ever since she was twelve months old, and is severely intellectually handicapped. Thomas and Klara believe her disability is due to a vaccine she received when eleven months old, and are very involved in anti-vaccination forums. We've intercepted a lot of internet traffic relating to a research facility in Berlin that has recently developed the first successful vaccine for M-fever.'

'That doesn't mean Thomas and Klara are going to do anything violent, though, does it?' I ask, trying to hide my conflicting emotions at the words *first successful vaccine*. I wonder what my father has to say about that. He should be happy, I guess.

'No, it doesn't, but not long ago Klara secured a part-time job as a cleaner for this facility, which seems odd given that she vehemently opposes everything that the research facility stands for. Currently we don't have enough information to pre-empt anything, but the pattern of escalating attacks means we need to be hypervigilant.'

Phoenix leans back in his chair. 'I assume that's where we come in.'

'You assume right,' Bauer says. I'm still staring at the family on the screen. Klara and Thomas don't look like terrorists. What if the ITA are wrong?

Phoenix's voice drops into the centre-swirl of my thoughts. *We don't look like spies, either.* Aloud, he says, 'So do they have a history of violent activity?'

Bauer shakes his head. 'No, but they belonged to an organisation that opposed animal testing in their youth, and were connected to members who bombed vivisectionists.'

'Do they have access to weapons?' I ask.

Bauer spreads his hands. 'I'm hoping you'll be able to tell us.'

'OK . . .' I frown as a new idea occurs to me. 'Won't the

customs retinal recognition software detect us as our former selves since we already have our own passports?'

'Well, no,' Bauer says.

Phoenix glances between Bauer and me. 'Why not?'

'Because,' Bauer says, 'your former selves have been erased. Have you got any more questions?'

By the time the setting sun melts into the horizon, I'm exhausted. Phoenix and I have spent the rest of the day memorising maps of Berlin, including the underground, practising our German, familiarising ourselves with our new micro-PAs, and undergoing a set of medical checks.

It's Melody who listens to my heart and lungs, Melody who takes my blood, Melody who transmits my heart's electrical activity to the ECG monitor and then takes me to another room for a WEB scan.

Even I can see all the new areas in my brain lighting up on the screen. The frontal lobes and temporal lobes, which control my speech, complex thinking and planning. The amygdala and hippocampus, which control my emotion and memory. The parietal lobes, which control movement and spatial awareness. The occipital lobes, my visual centres.

'Well,' Melody says, her fingers flying over the keys on her mini-Tab, 'you've come a long way since your last WEB scan.'

'Is that a surprise?'

'Not at all.' She sets aside the mini-Tab and removes the sticky dots from my forehead. 'It's just that it's . . .'

'Exponential?'

'Yes,' she says, touching her ear, as if she's worried I'm accessing her. I'm not — not even Ethan can overcome those now — but why not let her be a little bit rattled? 'Anyway, you've passed with flying colours. Be careful over there, and feel free to contact me if you need me.' She opens the door, but I don't leave. She may be finished with me, but I'm far from finished with her.

'Actually,' I say, 'there is something you can help me with.'

'So what did she say?' Ethan and I are floating in the pool, watching the stars appear in the night sky. Every time I close my eyes and open them, there are more, until it's as if the sky has been strewn with fairy dust. I wonder if my dream-flow could float up there, if I could escape the atmosphere and go into orbit.

The thought is exciting and terrifying, all at once.

'She gave me the injection,' I say. 'But she said it will be five days before it starts working.'

'Right.' I can sense Ethan's disappointment, but it's fleeting. 'It's OK,' he adds, brushing his hand past mine before switching to think-speak. *You will come back, won't you?*

Of course.

I wouldn't blame you, he says, *if you tried to escape. It wouldn't be that hard. You could tell them where we are.* But his colours are changing, orange-yellow as he realises why I'd never do that. I don't have to tell him. I don't have to, because I'm letting him access what Marlow said to me this afternoon, after Phoenix and I were given our micro-PAs.

You will have access to the Interweb. You can contact whomever you like. But I'd urge you to remember that if you reveal who you are and where you've come from, then you could put not just yourselves but every other member of VORTEX in jeopardy. Marlow had looked straight at me when he said that. I knew then that it was no accident that I had been chosen. If it hadn't been me, then they would have sent Ethan instead, but never, never, both of us.

How to guarantee the return of your pawns, Ethan think-says, resignedly. *But I wouldn't blame you if you didn't.*

No. I stand up. *When we do escape — and we will — we'll do it together. OK?*

Ethan draws me closer to him. 'OK,' he says, and neither of us speaks about the other thing, the bigger thing. He kisses me, his thought-stream becoming as opaque, as cloudy, as my own.

He's holding something back from me, I think.

But then, I'm withholding information from him, too.

Our lives depend on it.

THIRTY-SEVEN

ETHAN

I t's the twenty-third of December. Violet and Phoenix are leaving today. It could be the last time we ever see them. They could, despite everything Violet has said, decide to escape. They could be killed before they complete their mission.

I'm trying not to think about that, trying not to think about Violet being blown up or burned with acid.

And all Violet can talk about is my heart.

'I think it will be fine,' I say. We're lying tangled in bed. Both of us have woken early, five-thirty am. The sun has yet to explode above the horizon. 'We're so much stronger than we were when we arrived.' I kiss the side of her neck. 'You've probably healed me anyway.'

'We don't know that for sure.' Her eyes glitter at me. I'm tracing the curve of her collarbone with my tongue, dipping into the notch at the base of her throat.

'If you don't go to Berlin,' I say, 'then they'll just send me instead.'

'True.' Her breath quickens. 'Ethan . . .'

'Mmm?' I wish she'd stop talking. It's not helping. All I want is to be close to her for as long as possible, skin on skin, before all I have is her voice.

'Have you tried to contact Rawiri again?' she asks.

'Yeah.' At first I tried every day after I got here. Lately it's been once a week. The result is always the same — nothing. It makes me worry that something has happened to him, that the Foundation have found a way to shut him up. Or maybe it's just that my reach isn't wide enough. 'Maybe you can search up his name once you get Interweb access and see if you can find any reports of him missing.'

Violet inhales. 'I will. I can't wait to see what they've been saying about us.'

'Everyone will think we're dead, won't they?'

'Probably.' Her colour is pigeon-grey, seeping into my own confused mix of emotions. I move my lips to the space between her breasts. Violet stops talking. So do I. By the time we've finished, our colours have merged, yellow-green, and our thought-streams have changed from words to sensations.

Time slips past. The sun is rising. My heart is leaving.

We make a point of not saying goodbye.

At ten am, while I'm tumbling over Callum's shoulder in a martial arts session, Violet tells me she is boarding a plane at Alice Springs airport.

At three pm, halfway through a VirtReal simulation that requires us to solve complex mathematical proofs to break into a foreign government facility, Violet tells me she is flying over China.

Do you feel OK? she asks.

No, I'm already missing you like crazy, I think-reply.

You know what I mean.

I know what she means. *I feel fine,* I say, feeling the pulse at my wrist. Sixty beats per minute. Slow, strong, steady. *Stop worrying about me. Have they given you champagne? A foot massage?*

Yes to the champagne. No to the foot massage.

Dart's voice intrudes through my headphones. 'What's up, Wright, are you having a nap?'

'No.' I focus on the images in front of my goggles, rather than the image I still have of Violet this morning, her head tipped back, her throat tilted to my lips.

Got to go, I say. *See you soon.*

See you soon, she echoes, and then she's gone, but not gone.

As soon as the VirtReal sim ends, Dart tells me I'm needed for a medical.

'A medical?'

'Just routine,' he says, before taking me to one of the clinic rooms located in the centre of the spiral. Melody is waiting for me. I could almost attach the ECG dots to my chest by now, could almost read the ECG tracing myself.

'Looks good to me,' I say, watching the electrical peaks and valleys scroll across the screen.

'It does.' Melody turns off the screen, but holds up her hand when I go to remove one of the dots. 'Leave them on.' When I frown, she says, 'Doctor Griffin thought we should take a forty-eight-hour recording.'

'Why? I've been OK for ages.' Do *they* know about the connection between Violet and me? How can they?

Bland-faced, Melody says, 'It's a routine check. They're water-proof, so no problem if you want to shower or swim with them.'

I guess I should be grateful that the Foundation staff are looking out for me; grateful that if the connection between Violet and me is lost, any arrhythmia will be picked up straight away. Should be, but it makes me feel like a weakling, a liability.

We're halfway down the corridor when I hear someone say, 'Why, hello, Melody.' It's a woman I haven't seen before with short, raspberry-red hair.

Slowing, Melody says, 'Hi, Greta. What brings you here?'

'Bit of this, bit of that. Research, I guess you could call it.' Greta flashes her teeth at me. 'And you are . . .'

'Ethan,' I say, noting that (a) there is no blocking device in her ear, unless she's got some sort of miniature version and (b) how Melody is trying to warn her off with her eyes. At least, I think that's what she's doing, but she's too late because I'm getting the blue flare of her thought-stream. Or am I confusing her memories with my own? Because I'm seeing a room with a row of pods, just like in the dream I had while recovering from M-fever. I'm seeing staff wearing protective gowns and masks and goggles. I'm hearing *attenuated virus* and *WEB scan* and *feeling our way blind*.

'I was hoping to have a brief chat, when you're free,' Greta says to Melody.

'Now is good,' Melody says, before practically frog-marching her to the lift. 'Catch you later, Ethan.'

'Catch you,' I say, watching Melody press the button for One Below. I watch them step into the lift. I wait as they descend to the floor that we've been told is for administration and staff, the floor the retinal recognition pads won't let the members of VORTEX anywhere near.

I stay where I am by the window, watching dark clouds

billow outside. As hard as I concentrate, I can't hear Greta anymore. Presumably Melody has found her a blocking device or the equivalent, whatever that might be.

I think I understand what's happening in the dream that isn't a dream though. If I'm right, the Foundation is running experiments that would stack right up there with those conducted by Nazi Germany in World War II: infecting teenagers with the M-fever virus in order to create more of us. My heart should be racing right now, but the pendulum beat in my ears continues unaltered. Strong. Slow. Steady.

I send out thought-tendrils, seeking the others. The collective, my fellow VORTEX members, are horsing around in the pool. As for anyone else, anyone like us, I can't find them.

Not yet.

THIRTY-EIGHT:

VIOLET

t's cold when we arrive in Berlin, snowflakes swirling through the grey morning air. It's early morning here, Christmas Eve. I've lost track of what time it should be in Central Australia, let alone New Zealand. I'm tired and my eyes are gritty, and I don't know if what I'm feeling is fatigue or hunger or homesickness or all three.

'We've loaded plenty of money onto your PAs, so you should be able to buy anything you need,' Bruno says, once we've cleared customs. 'Your apartment has been stocked with the basic items. Any problems, call me.' He takes his PA out of the pocket of his winter coat and frowns at the screen. 'I'd better get going, my flight to Munich leaves in half an hour. Good luck.' He takes off, lifting the PA to his ear.

We exit the terminal and wheel our suitcases over to the queue for a Zuber, shivering in the sub-zero air. Phoenix looks different in his black beanie and Supa Puffa jacket.

You look different too, he think-says. I guess I do, with my fur-lined hood and snow boots.

'And your lips are blue,' Phoenix adds, jogging up to a Zuber as its exiting occupants drag their suitcases out of the boot.

'Danke,' I say, when one of the men holds the passenger door open for me.

'Bitte.' The man smiles and turns to help his companion with her suitcase. He's thinking I'm quite — what?

Attractive, Phoenix supplies, sliding into the seat beside me.

Flushing, I think-say, *I keep forgetting how we'll be able to read everyone now.* Now that they're not wearing blocking devices, that is.

We hope. Phoenix types our location into his PA and the Zuber noses into the line of traffic. I bring up the web browser on my own PA and type in the name I've been dying to search for the last couple of months: my own.

There aren't as many news items as I thought there would be. The first link reads: *Nicholas Black and family grieve after their only child dies from M-fever relapse.*

'M-fever relapse?' I tap on the link.

'Huh?' Phoenix glances at me. 'Oh. Right. Well, you didn't think they'd report *real* news, did you?'

Ignoring him, I read on. *The body of Nicholas Black's daughter Violet has been found several metres off a bush track in West Auckland. The 17-year-old was reported missing five days ago. It is believed that she had a seizure related to an M-fever relapse and stopped breathing. Nicholas Black and his wife have declined to comment.*

I don't know why I feel so weird when I read that — it's no more than I expected — but reading about my own death makes me wonder if I've split off another version of myself, a doppelgänger.

'Have you looked yourself up yet?' I ask Phoenix.

'No.' He's tapping and swiping on his PA, though. 'Listen to

197

this. *Next generation M-fever vaccines given to hundreds of children in New Zealand and Australia*. Dated nineteenth of December.'

'Five days ago.' Yet again, I wonder what my father has to say about that. I'm not sure I want to know. As tempting as it is to contact my parents, I know I can't. Not when every call, every internet search I make is being tracked, monitored, logged. Marlow's words are still fresh in my memory: *I'd urge you to remember that if you reveal who you are and where you've come from, then you could put not just yourselves but every other member of VORTEX in jeopardy.*

'So, a vaccine.' Phoenix slips the PA into his jacket pocket. 'Guess there won't be too many more of us, then.'

'Guess not.' I've moved on to the next post. 'Oh. Listen to this. The bodies of . . .' I swallow, 'Ethan Wright, Violet Black, Audrey Spelling, Harper Mehta, Callum Templeman and Jonathan (Johnno) Fletcher were laid to rest today. Bodies — what the hell?'

Phoenix peers over my shoulder. 'As per health authority regulations, the bodies were buried in closed caskets due to the risk of infection.' He snorts. 'Bet the families weren't allowed to see the so-called dead bodies either. Like I said, fake news.'

'But . . . who's Jonathan?' For once Phoenix isn't blocking me, although I can tell from the silver blur of his emotions that he'd like to. *Johnno*, I say, switching to think-speak. *Is that—*

That's me. Phoenix fingers the Japanese characters above his left eyebrow, averts his eyes. *Or was.*

You changed your name? The noise of the road beneath the car changes, and I hear the whirr of tyres on cobblestones.

After my sister died. I guess I was trying to . . . forget. Reinvent myself.

Phoenix rising, I say.

From the ashes, yeah, that's the one. His lips curl upward. *Unless you're a Black Wolf, that is.*

Wolf Schwarz. Liesl Meyer. I trace an L in the condensation on my window. Insipid sun sneaks through grubby clouds. It has stopped snowing. I look at my PA again. Perhaps I could write my parents a letter. The Foundation couldn't track *that . . .* could they?

As soon as the thought flits through my mind, my heart starts racing so fast I can hardly breathe, and my stomach clenches so tightly I feel sick.

Phoenix touches my shoulder. *Are you all right?*

Yeah, I'm . . . I inhale, shake my head. *Fine. Just fine.* I haven't had a panic attack before, but if I did, I think this is what it would feel like.

'Let's go to the Christmas market,' Phoenix says in German.

'I want to have a shower,' I reply, also in German. 'And put some warmer clothes on.' *And don't we have work to do?*

Phoenix think-says, *Bruno said we should spend the first day orientating ourselves.* Aloud, he says, 'We should go for a walk, try and stay awake. It'll help with the jet lag.'

'OK,' I reply. 'Und Kaffee,' I add.

I've never really drunk much coffee before, but I think I could do with some now.

'I can't believe they only got us a one-bedroom apartment.' I flop onto the couch. One bedroom with a queen-sized bed, one bathroom, a tiny lounge and kitchen.

'We're poor students, remember?' Phoenix opens the fridge, closes it again. 'I'll take the couch.'

'You've got longer legs than me. I can sleep on the couch.'

'I got in first.' He gives me a half-grin before strolling into the bathroom and closing the door. Moving over to the window, I peer down on the street below. Just like at home, most of the cars are Zubers, but I can still see the occasional BMW or Audi with an elderly driver behind the wheel. The pedestrians are wearing hats, fur-lined coats, scarfs, boots. Hard to believe that, yesterday, I was in a red desert with temperatures set to climb to forty degrees Celsius.

Behind me, Phoenix says, 'You can shower first if you want, since I got first dibs on the couch.'

'Very funny.' I turn. He's kicked his shoes off and is lying on the bed, his hands behind his head. 'Don't get too comfortable there.'

'I won't,' he says, but when I emerge from the bathroom fifteen minutes later, his eyes are closed, his breathing slow. I flop down next to him, hoping the motion of the bed will wake him up, but he doesn't stir. Turning onto my side, I whisper, 'Wolf,' and then, 'Johnno.'

'I didn't mean it,' he mumbles, which doesn't make sense, but maybe that's because I called him by his childhood name. Maybe he's dreaming of the past life he's been trying so hard to forget.

And it's so warm in here, and the bed is surprisingly comfortable, so I close my eyes, too.

'Liesl.' A hand on my shoulder, a whiff of coffee. *Violet.*

I blink. 'Oh. God. What time is it?'

'Lunch time.' Phoenix, who is crouching beside the bed, straightens up. It takes me a split second to realise he's speaking in German, and another split second to register where I am.

Berlin. ITA. Ethan.

'Would you like a coffee? I found these.' He holds up a box of coffee capsules with flavours like hazelnut and mocha listed on the outside. 'There's a machine in the kitchen.'

'OK. Thanks.' I swing my legs over the side of the bed. 'And then I think . . . I'm hungry.'

After drinking the coffee so fast I nearly strip the lining off my throat — I can't wait to explore — we bundle up in our hats, coats, scarfs and gloves and take three flights of stairs to the ground level. Tonight the Neumanns will return from a trip to Munich. Until then, we have a day to *orientate ourselves*, as Bruno instructed, before trying to ferret out enough information to potentially prevent hundreds of doctors and scientists from being killed and maimed.

A day to play, I think, then feel guilty for even thinking of having fun when Ethan and the others are still trapped in the middle of the Australian desert. So I try to tell myself I'm not having fun. I'm not.

After buying pretzels from a street vendor, we wander through a park, our breath ghosting in front of us.

'Look at that.' I grab Phoenix's sleeve and point. His eyes are following the animal already, which is scurrying up a tree. 'What do you think it is? A squirrel?'

'Or a fox.' Phoenix tears off a chunk of pretzel. A guy in a long overcoat walks past us, and I intercept his thought-stream for a few seconds, long enough to learn that he is debating what to have for dinner.

You know what, I think-say, *most people's thoughts are not that interesting.*

Yeah, it's mostly random garbage. We're crossing a bridge. Ahead of us, a pair of girls race each other on e-snow scooters, their laughter trailing behind them. Phoenix stops halfway across and leans over the railing. *Have you ever seen a frozen pond?*

No. Wow. In contrast to the grey-white surroundings, the pond is pea-green, presumably from algae. I'm thinking of stories where someone goes walking or skating on a frozen lake and has fallen through the ice. That would be my worst nightmare, floating beneath the surface, trying to break my way free.

'Yeah?' Phoenix turns his head. 'That's your worst nightmare?'

'I think so. What's yours?'

'Burning to death. At least if you drown, it's not painful.'

'How do you know *that*?'

'I don't. But I figure once your brain is deprived of oxygen for long enough, then you just black out. Burning is super-painful. Apparently.'

'Ugh.' I shiver, and Phoenix says, 'Let's find some better coffee, shall we?'

We find our coffee. We also find the giant-sized Brandenburg Gate and the hundred-year-old Reichstag. Berlin is a jewel, with Christmas lights adorning trees and buildings, sparkling winged horses and bears and carolers whose voices are as clear and glassy as the frigid air. When we walk past the store windows, the e-displays change, tempting us with designer clothes, e-skis, micro-Tabs and the latest PAs. Everything a seventeen- and nineteen-year-old could want — unless you're virally optimised, that is. All I want is to go home and to be with Ethan. Right now, I'm a long way off having either of those things.

'Hey,' Phoenix says, once we've reached Alexanderplatz. 'Let's have a go on that.'

'Are you kidding?' I eye up the man-made ski slope, on which a couple of kids are hurtling down on plastic trays. 'I can't ski.'

'It's just a toboggan. You can sit on a toboggan, can't you?'

'It's all your fault if I break both my arms.'

You can heal yourself, can't you?

I have no idea.

'Hmm.' Phoenix draws away, gives me a contemplative look.

I gesture at the street vendors. *Ever had mulled wine?*

No. Phoenix digs his PA out of his pocket. 'Two mulled wines, coming right up.'

The mulled wine tastes just as good as it smells, like cinnamon and cloves and berries. I cup my glass, taking in the Christmas lights and carols and laughter and kids bundled up in their down jackets and hats and mittens, and the snow, which has just begun to fall again, soft like butterflies on my cheeks, and I feel as though my world just got a whole lot bigger.

Me too, Phoenix think-says. It's not even bothering me anymore, how he keeps slipping in and out of my thought-stream like that. We perch side-by-side on a pair of stools with heated seats, watching the world go by. I'm not sure if I'm a little bit drunk or just really jet lagged, but at some point I rest my head on Phoenix's shoulder and he slips an arm around my back. If I had to explain how I feel right now, it would be content and safe, even though I'm about to embark on the most dangerous thing I've ever done.

Once we've finished our drinks, Phoenix says, 'How about that toboggan?'

'Are you trying to kill me?'

'Would I do that?'

'I don't know.' I stand up and nearly fall over.

Phoenix laughs. 'OK, Liesl, time for dinner and bed.'

Was that meant to be some kind of come-on? I think-say as we leave Alexanderplatz behind us, weaving only ever-so-slightly.

You know what I mean. We're acting, remember?

Sure, I think-reply, ignoring the tiny stab of guilt in my chest, vowing to talk to Ethan as soon as we return to the apartment. *Because if you try to get in bed with me, I'll punch you. Just saying.*

'A woman after my own heart,' he murmurs, taking my hand. When I stiffen, he think-says, *Acting, remember? We have no idea who's watching us. We have to play our part.*

I remember, I think-say. *I remember.*

THIRTY-NINE

ETHAN

Christmas Eve comes and goes, and I don't hear from Violet the whole time. It's not because she's out of reach — we're so much stronger than we used to be, so much more adept at fixing on those we want to communicate with, especially when they're fellow VORTEX members. Yet when I try to chat to her, just after dinner, all I get is the slow blue undulation I associate with sleep. By my calculations, it's mid-morning in Berlin.

I don't want to wake her, and I can't exactly leave a message, so I go for a swim instead. Length after length, my limbs slicing through the night-black water, and I know this: Violet is with me, even now. I can hear her heart in my ears, feel her breath in my lungs. Our twin heartbeats speed up as I swim twenty, thirty laps. I wonder if she senses that in her sleep, or if she is oblivious. I wonder how cold it is over there, if it's snowing. I wonder if I can trust Phoenix to keep her safe.

An hour later, I sit on the side of the pool, my muscles aching, a hollow sensation in my belly.

I miss you, Vi, I whisper, but she doesn't reply.

It's just after three and I'm wide awake. It's not just Violet's absence that is stopping me from going to sleep. I can't stop thinking about the faceless people in the pods.

Attenuated virus. WEB scan. Feeling our way blind.

When I tried to bring it up with Audrey earlier today, she'd thought-said, *That could mean anything. Maybe they're trying to make a vaccine. Is that such a bad thing?*

Harper had thought-said, *So what if they're carrying out experiments? What are we going to do about it, anyway?*

Callum hadn't taken part in the conversation. He was too immersed in the VirtReal game he's been playing in every second of his spare time, Alternative Universe. I wonder how Rawiri is getting on without my ideas for our game. Maybe he's canned it now I've gone. A new fear grips me: what if Rawiri is one of the innocent people the Foundation may or may not be experimenting on? What if they're trying to create more of us?

There's a humming in my ears, and a voice cuts through my rapid-fire thought-stream.

Ethan? Are you awake?

Violet. Hey. I'm so excited I sit bolt upright. *How are you? What are you doing? What's Berlin like?*

I feel rather than hear her laughter, warm and yellow, like sunshine. *Slow down. I'm fine. It's freezing here, but it's beautiful.* Then *she's* the one talking a mile a minute about frozen ponds and rivers and snow and Christmas lights. I'm happy for her but I'm jealous too.

I wish I could be there with you, I think-say.

I wish you could too. What time is it over there?

I check the glowing digits on the clock beside my bed. *Ten past three.*

Ten past three? In the morning? Oh my God. I'm so sorry. I've totally screwed up the time difference. I don't think my brain's working anymore.

It's OK. I was awake.

Waiting for me, she says before I can block *that* thought. *I'm sorry I didn't try to talk to you earlier.*

It's all right. You were busy.

Well, Merry Christmas. She hesitates. *I should let you go to sleep.*

No, I think-say. *Don't leave. Have you found* them *yet?*

The terrorists? No. We were so tired today, and we didn't want to screw it up. We're going to wander past where they live tomorrow, see if we can intercept anything.

Be careful.

We will.

And I do block her then, because I don't want Violet to hear how I wish she wouldn't say *we* all the time, as though she and Phoenix are part of a secret club. I'm not jealous, I tell myself. I'm not.

But I am.

Ethan, if I could have chosen . . .

I know. It's OK. I take a deep breath. *Hey. I need to tell you something.*

What's that?

I tell her about meeting Greta, about how I think the Foundation might be trying to infect more teenagers with the M-fever virus to create more of us.

But . . . that's horrible. Violet's disgust-horror is khaki-green. *Where do you think they get these teenagers from?*

I don't know. I don't even know if they're teenagers. They could be prisoners for all I know, or volunteers.

Who would volunteer for that? *Most will die.*

Poor people? I think-suggest.

Maybe. So what are you going to do?

I don't know yet. I guess I need more information. How I'm going to get that, I have no idea. *I'm missing you like crazy.*

Me too. I'm counting down the days until I can see you again.

But how many days is that? I think-ask.

Well, she think-says. *If we can flush out enough evidence over the next few days, then the ITA can arrest the suspects and whoever else they're collaborating with, and we can come back.*

You make it sound so easy. Why doesn't she sound even the least bit frightened? Maybe it's harder for me, because I'm sitting here doing nothing.

Violet think-says, gently, *You're not doing nothing, Ethan. If you're right, then there might be some people who desperately need our help.*

I rake my fingers through my hair. *But how can we help them if we can't even help ourselves?*

It's only a matter of time, Violet think-says. *You know how I know that?* And now we're communicating without words again. She's showing me images of the two of us in a foreign city with cobblestone streets and ancient buildings, and in this dream or premonition or whatever it is, we're sitting side-by-side, Violet holding my bleeding wrist because she has just cut out my implant. No more tracking. No more ITA. Just the two of us, free to do anything we want.

We're already smarter than them, she think-says. *Please don't worry about me. Just look after yourself.* Her thought-images have changed again: no, not just thoughts, but sensations.

Oh, I think-say. *Wow.* This is what Violet feels like when I'm kissing her. This is how her skin tingles when I stroke her belly, her breasts, her inner thighs. In return, I show her how it feels when *I'm* pressed against *her*, all the way down, and before I know it, I'm seeing starbursts behind my eyelids. Whoa.

It's not quite as good as the real thing, but it's close.

Sleep well, Ethan, Violet says. *And remember: together, we are infinite.*

Together, we are infinite, I echo. I roll over, hug my pillow to my chest. *Love you, Violet*, I think-whisper, and smile myself to sleep.

FORTY:

VIOLET

The following morning, I wake at four am. No surprise, I guess, considering it's twelve-thirty pm in Darwin. It's amazing that I slept as long as I did. I slide out of bed, wrapping the duvet around me, and pad over to the window.

'Wow,' I whisper. More snow has fallen overnight, thick layers blanketing the street and the tops of the buildings. It seems to have muted all the sound, or perhaps it's just that the rest of Berlin is asleep.

'I don't think Berlin ever sleeps, does it?' Phoenix says from behind me. 'We could go to a nightclub.'

'That's the last thing I feel like doing.'

'Are you going back to sleep, or can I turn on the light?'

'You can turn on the light,' I say, tracing a shape in the condensation on the window.

'What's with the pyramid?' Phoenix slopes into the kitchen and flicks the switch on the side of the coffee machine.

'It's the complete opposite of a spiral.' I'd be happy if I never saw a spiral logo again.

'Well, in a geometrical sense, a line is the complete—' Phoenix holds up his hands. 'Hey, I was joking, OK?'

'Smart arse,' I grumble. Once he has made our coffee, I ask, 'So how come you joined the army?' I'm sitting cross-legged on the bed, the duvet still wrapped around me.

'Why does anyone join the army?' Phoenix sits on the couch, pushing his blanket aside.

'Because they like guns?' When he rolls his eyes at me, I say, 'OK, because they want to defend their country.'

He shakes his head. 'Wrong. Most recruits join because they need the money.'

I chew my lower lip. 'Oh. Right. That makes sense, I guess.'

'The army were going to pay for my engineering degree. I was earning enough to pay for my sister's board and school uniform, enough to make us independent.' He takes a slug of coffee, wipes his mouth. 'And then she got sick.' His thought-stream is blue-grey again, so intense the melancholy is seeping into me, too.

'Her name was Tilly, right?'

'Yeah.' Phoenix is gripping his mug so tightly his knuckles have turned white. 'I didn't know how sick she was until Francine, the lady she boarded with, rang to tell me Tilly had been in bed all week. Francine was scared to go too close to her in case she caught something. By the time I got to the house, Tilly was so far gone she couldn't even talk.' His breathing hitches. 'I took her to hospital and they put her on life support, but it was too late. A week after she died, I lay in bed at the army camp, burning up with fever. My roommate said, *Dude, you need to go to hospital*. I asked him to leave me alone. I just wanted to die.'

'But you didn't.' I wait for Phoenix to carry on, but he doesn't. A black silence settles upon the room. Outside, the snow is still falling, softly, softly. I stand up and move to sit beside him.

Touch him, tentatively, on the knee. 'Do you wish you'd died?'

Phoenix presses his fingers against the tattoo above his eyebrow. 'I used to.'

'And now?'

He swings his eyes towards me. 'At least now I have a purpose. I even have a family, sort of.'

'You mean VORTEX?'

'Of course.' He stands up, stretching. 'Are you hungry?'

'Starving,' I say.

'Then,' he says, pulling items out of the cupboards and fridge — mixing bowls, along with flour, milk and eggs — 'you're in for a treat. Hope you like pancakes.'

I curl my legs beneath me. 'I love pancakes.' I pick up my PA and think, yet again, of how easy it would be to send my parents or one of my friends a message, even if it were an anonymous one, to tell them where I am. Seconds later, I leap up and run to the toilet, just in time to bring up the contents of my stomach.

'Urrgh. God.' I run a shaking hand over my lips.

'Are you all right?' Phoenix hovers behind me.

'Yeah, I . . .' I rub my chest. Slow down, heart, slow down. Why is my body going into alert mode every time I think of getting hold of anyone from my past life?

Even *that* thought is enough to start me dry-retching again. Phoenix crouches beside me, rubbing between my shoulder blades.

'You should go have a lie down,' he says, once I've managed to regain my composure, sort of.

'No,' I say, standing up to rinse my mouth out. 'No, I think it was just a . . . passing thing.'

But I wonder. I wonder, I wonder.

A couple of hours later, I sit on the couch, turning my gun over in my hands. It's not loaded — yet — but it will be before we leave the apartment.

You'll find your weapons in the safe in the wardrobe, Bauer had told us. *The keypad is programmed to recognise your fingerprints.*

Better not lose our hands, then, Phoenix had replied. Bauer hadn't laughed. I wasn't sure whether to be worried by that.

Setting the gun down on the arm of the couch, I cross the room to take my bullet-proof vest out of my suitcase. It's thinner than I expected, a centimetre at the most. The latest technology, according to Dash. After shucking off my jersey, I pull the vest over my head and tighten the straps around the sides.

Phoenix exits the bathroom, his toothbrush sticking out of his mouth. 'Looking slick, Black.'

'*You're* the Black, Wolf.' *Black Wolf. Phoenix rising. Johnno Fletcher.* I'm losing track of all of his names. 'I'm Liesl Meyer, remember?'

'Liesl, weasel,' he says in English, and I'm half-expecting him to take me by the hand and spin me around, he's in such an ebullient mood. Quite a shift from a couple of hours before, when we were talking about how he'd wished he were dead.

'You're enjoying this, aren't you?'

'Aren't *you*?' Phoenix counters, and I hesitate before deciding there's no point in lying.

I reach for the gun, take the bullets off the bench. 'Beats being trapped in the middle of the desert,' I say, keeping my voice even. *I'm not terrified. I'm not.* And if I can stop who knows how many innocent people from being detonated, from being deterred in their mission to stop the M-fever epidemic, then I'll feel as though I'm worth something.

No, more than that. I'll feel powerful. Needed. And capable of carrying out the next task, and the next.

I slide the bullets into the left-inside pocket of my jacket, the gun into the right one. *Are you ready?*

Ready, Phoenix think-says.

It's quarter past six when we leave the apartment. The city is still quiet, barely another pedestrian in sight, empty Zubers parked along both sides of the street. I let Phoenix take my hand, even though it feels weird in all sorts of ways. We're actors in a play, I tell myself.

A play that could have deadly consequences.

'This way,' Phoenix says, not even consulting his PA before leading me down the steps to the underground. Like me, he has committed the map of Central Berlin to memory, along with the underground network that connects the city. Seconds after we've stepped onto the platform, an M-Bahn slides into the station. There is only one other person in the carriage, an elderly man who looks like a grubby version of Santa Claus.

Someone's had too many eggnogs, Phoenix think-says, taking a seat as far away as possible from the Claus lookalike.

He's got a tough job, I think-reply, and get a smile in return. Slipping my hand out of Phoenix's grasp, I gaze out of the window, reading the graffiti on the walls as the train gathers speed. *Gretel loves Thomas. Screw the French. Screw the government. Screw me please, I'm horny.* I can't help laughing at that last one.

A few stops later, we alight at Zoo Station and take the travellator up to the street level. The sun is out, but there's no warmth in it, and the wind is so cold it hurts to take a deep breath. I wrap my scarf around the lower half of my face and reach for

Phoenix's hand. A happy, carefree couple out for a Christmas morning stroll. No one can tell my heart is racing.

Our heart. I wonder what Ethan is doing, wonder if he can feel the adrenaline surging through my arteries. I wonder how it can be possible that I'm supporting his heart from the other side of the world. But I can't think about him right now. I need to concentrate, need to fix on our targets.

Phoenix halts outside an apartment block with alternating red and blue floors. *Stairs or lift?*

Stairs, I think-say, so we climb four flights and pause in the stairwell. Thomas and Klara's apartment is only a few metres away. I stare out of the window, my gaze turning inward as I intercept a new thought-stream. It is in German.

Can't even open her own presents . . . should have gone to Mutter and Vater's after all . . . happy when this day is over . . .

Nothing too earth-shattering coming from Klara, I think.

Phoenix raises an eyebrow at me. *Like you said, most people's thoughts are not that interesting.*

I snort and lean against the wall. *And the movies make out espionage to be so exciting.*

Nah, most of the time it must be dull as Marlow on a first date.

How do you know he's dull on a first date?

Phoenix smirks at me. *How do you know he's not?*

Strangling a giggle, I try to concentrate on our task. *I can't believe you're joking at a time like this.*

No one said we shouldn't, Phoenix retorts, but he's turning his head, tuning in again. I close my eyes, concentrating on doing the same.

Dying for a smoke . . . wish I hadn't agreed to meet Dieter for lunch tomorrow . . . arrogant pig . . .

A door bangs. Before I have time to react, Phoenix spins me around and pins me against the wall.

Relax, he think-says, and presses his lips against mine. Behind us, I hear footsteps, sense a thought-stream tinged with irritation.

Thinks I'm stupid, the man is thinking. *Show that patronising prick . . . wish those two would take that somewhere else . . .*

I can't relax, not when someone is thinking angry thoughts about me, not when Phoenix is kissing me like—

Phoenix releases me, steps away. *Sorry.*

Pressing my palms to my scorching cheeks, I glance away. Thomas Neumann has gone, his footsteps barely audible but his thoughts still crashing into my skull.

Wait until they realise their Javier broth has gone missing . . . try and vaccinate their way out of that . . .

Did you hear that? I think-ask, still unable to look at Phoenix.

Yeah. Phoenix pinches his nostrils, not looking at me either. *But it's not evidence. We need something solid, not just fantasies.*

I frown, but I know he's right. More haste, less speed, as my mum always likes to tell me. We've got a fix on our suspects now, can track them whenever we want.

Exactly. Phoenix starts down the stairs, and I follow him, tuning back into Klara. But it's not Klara I hear, it's her daughter.

Mummy sad Mummy sad Mummy sad. Mia's colour is grey, grey, grey.

'Liesl,' Phoenix says, and I realise I've come to a standstill, gripping the railing as if I'm about to tip into the stairwell.

'Coming,' I answer, but I don't move, not until Phoenix takes me by the arm.

No, he think-says, as I fight an almost overwhelming wave of melancholy, *I don't think you can heal her disability.*

Before I can ask how he can be so sure, he adds, *Come on, let's get as far away from this place as possible. It's giving me the creeps.*

He's not joking. It's his dread I'm feeling now, shivery and purple.

What's up? I ask as we leave the red and blue building behind us.

Are you kidding? Do you know what Javier virus can do to you?

I slow. *Of course, do you think I'm stupid?*

Phoenix's sigh is visible, a white puff of breath. *I think you know exactly what I'm thinking, Vi.*

Not wanting to challenge him on that — because I never know *exactly* what he's thinking — I say, *Javier virus is like Ebola on steroids.* My dad was fascinated when the first reports of a new virus came out a few years ago. I remembered watching the documentary with him. *They named the virus after the scientist who discovered it.*

Poor bastard. He died, right?

I dig my chin into the top of my jacket. *Yeah, he bled to death. The mortality rate is eighty to ninety percent,* I add, determined to know more than Phoenix about something for once. *And it's super-contagious.*

Phoenix steps aside for a mother pushing a pram with an inflatable blanket domed over it. *But why would a Holistic want to spread a deadly disease like that?*

They're against vaccination because they think it injured their daughter, I point out. *That doesn't mean they're Holistic. And Thomas didn't say he wanted to spread it. Maybe we'll find out more when he meets with this Dieter guy tomorrow.*

I don't know, Thomas didn't seem to like Dieter much. But sure, let's fix on him then. Phoenix picks up the pace.

Where are you going so fast? I protest, jogging to catch up with him.

'To the Tiergarten,' he says aloud.

'Why?'

'Come on, Vi, it's Christmas Day. Let's have some fun — do you remember how to do that?'

'Oh,' I say, 'fun.' And then I'm laughing, and I'm relieved too, because his colour is soft and orange and he's hardly ever like that, ever.

And why am I noticing that, why?

Maybe it's wrong to have fun when Ethan is stuck in the middle of the desert, missing me. Maybe it's wrong to have fun when my parents are spending their first Christmas without me, believing my body is six feet under in a sealed coffin. But the alternative is to sit around feeling sorry for myself, or getting all wound up about how we're going to get enough evidence for the ITA to arrest Thomas and Klara.

'Ever made a snowman?' Phoenix asks when we reach the Tiergarten. Ducks are skidding around on the frozen surface of the moss-green pond, quacking in a semi-pissed-off kind of way. The air is still, crystalline.

'No. Have you?'

'Nope.' Phoenix drops into a crouch and starts scooping snow between his gloved hands. I bend over to scoop my own snow and roll it into my first-ever snowball. There's never any snow in Auckland, or anywhere in the North Island for that matter, not for at least the past ten years.

'Hey, Wolf,' I say. He's barely had time to turn before my snowball hits him in the ear.

'Hey!' His comeback is swift, a snowball between my shoulder blades. Giggling, I land one in the centre of his chest and go to run away. Before I know what's happening, I'm lying staring up at the sky, trying to draw a breath. Damn, I hadn't even seen that patch of ice.

Phoenix's face comes into view. 'You all right?'

'Yeah, I think I'm—' And before *he* knows what's happening, I've flipped him over and am sitting astride him, my knees on his elbows. I'm no match for his strength, I know that, but I'm enjoying the expression on his face.

'You little tart,' he says and flips me over, just like we practised in martial arts class, but only holding me by one wrist. I grab more snow and mush it into his lips. Phoenix splutters and grasps my other wrist, pinning me so I can't move. 'Watch it, Liesl.'

'No, *you* watch it,' I say, and suddenly my heart's beating way too fast, and he's blocking me but not fast enough. Not. Fast. Enough.

Phoenix releases me, springs to his feet. *It's not what you think,* he think-says.

It's a lie, and we both know it.

FORTY-ONE:

ETHAN

On Christmas morning, I wake to find a stocking hanging on a hook attached to the outside of my door. The curlicue letters stitched on top say: *Ethan*. When I peer down the corridor, I see the others have identical stockings.

'Huh.' I carry the stocking into my room and sit on my bed. The first item I draw out is a licorice wheel. Yum. After biting the end off the wheel, I reach into the stocking again, feeling like a little kid. Chewy caramels, a pair of see-in-the-dark swimming googles, a novel from the Scholastic millennium collection. This last is the first novel in the *Hunger Games* series, which is about a bunch of teenagers trying to kill each other. Is that meant to be some kind of hint?

Next is a perfectly spherical orange object with dimpled skin. I stare at the fruit for a moment. Definitely genetically engineered, since the Citrus Blight ravaged all our limes, lemons and oranges five years ago. Still, I'm curious to taste it. Will it be like the oranges I remember from kindergarten?

Audrey's voice is morning-clear. *It's good*, she think-says. *Just like the real thing.*

It is the real thing, Callum chimes in. *It tastes like sunshine.*

And I'm thinking, *No, kissing Violet is like tasting sunshine* and I'm missing her like hell, when there's a loud rap on my door. I know who it is before I fling it open because her thought-stream is so damn loud.

'So, you like your Christmas present,' I say, stepping aside to let her in.

Harper brushes past me and sits on my bed with a thud. 'Oh my God, this is gold.' She's holding the micro-PA as if it's — yeah, gold. 'Did you get one too?'

'I don't know.' I fish the last present out of the stocking, a small rectangular object wrapped in silver foil. 'Actually, probably, yeah.'

I peel the wrapping off. My micro-PA is identical to Harper's, apart from the colour. Hers is gold. Mine is lime-green.

'I haven't used the internet in, like, months,' Harper says.

'As if they'll let us use *that*,' I say, but to my surprise the web browser *is* working. What the hell, do the Foundation think we're trustworthy or something?

Harper groans. 'For God's sake.'

'What?'

'My email isn't working.'

'Well, *that's* a surprise.' I'm reading the latest news items. *Pharmaceutical company Präzision struggles to keep up with supply of M-fever vaccinations. King William delivers his Christmas Eve message, amid rumours his marriage is on the rocks. High-level terrorist alert across Europe as New Year's Eve approaches.*

'Or Hash Tag,' she carries on. 'Or any social media for that matter.'

'Who cares about social media?'

Changing to think-speak, Harper says, *You can send messages on social media, duh.*

As if they'd let us do that. I'm having fun surfing the net, though, until I find the article featuring my own funeral. *Seen this?* I show Harper the photo of concrete being poured on top of our sealed coffins.

Harper's mouth falls open. 'Oh my God. That's just . . . horrid.' A strange noise escapes her, and I realise she's suddenly, unexpectedly, crying.

I touch her shoulder. 'Well, you know, I'm not surprised.'

She's trembling. *We're never going to get out of here, are we?*

That's not true. They let Violet and Phoenix go to Berlin.

Yeah, but they're still prisoners. She squints at her PA again. *Ethan?*

Yeah?

Have you heard of a game called Eternity?

What? I grab the PA off her and stare open-mouthed at the headline: *VirtReal game designed by teenagers goes viral one week after being released.*

'Your name is there,' Harper says.

'Yeah, no kidding.'

'I could do without the sarcasm, Wright.'

Ignoring her, I read the first paragraph of the article. *A game that has been released weeks after its 17-year-old creators, Rawiri Sullivan and Ethan Wright, died of complications of M-fever . . .*

'Oh no.' A lead weight settles in the middle of my chest. *No, no, no.*

'What's — oh.' Harper pats me awkwardly on the arm. 'I'm sorry.'

'Yeah, me too.' No, I'm not just sorry, I'm guilty as hell. I might as well have put a noose around my best friend's neck and hung him from the highest tree. If I hadn't contacted him, he'd be alive now.

M-fever, yeah, right.

'It's not your fault,' Harper says, because obviously my thoughts are thunder-loud, ready for anyone to hear. Anyone who's virally optimised, that is.

'Virally optimised,' I whisper, before making myself read the rest of the article, even though the words have gone all blurry. *A game that has been released weeks after its 17-year-old creators, Rawiri Sullivan and Ethan Wright, died of complications of M-fever has also gone viral — with fans stating that Eternity is 'compulsive', 'exhilarating' and 'next level'. The deceased boys' parents have asked that all earnings from the game be donated to medical research.*

Damn it, what is my mother thinking? We're not exactly rich.

Harper peers over my shoulder. 'Wow. You didn't tell me you were an IT genius.'

'I'm not, Rawiri is.' Was. God. I feel sick. 'I just made up the characters, and the story.' Compulsive? Next level? I knew the game was good but . . . that good?

Something is off, but I can't figure out what.

'That's awesome.'

I toss the PA onto my pillow. 'It's not awesome, Harper. I killed my best friend, and our game is going viral and neither of us is going to benefit in the slightest. Ever.'

'That's not true,' Harper says, her voice wavering again. Crap. Man, I wish Violet was here. I wish I could talk to her. Instead, I sit beside Harper again, take a couple of deep breaths.

'I didn't mean to yell at you. It was just a shock, that's all.'

She crosses her arms. 'I'm sorry I'm not Violet.'

'I'm not sure you want to be Violet,' I mumble, making an effort to block her before she takes offence at any more of my thoughts.

'Don't I?' She stands up. 'Let me see, she's got a boyfriend, and she got to swan off to Berlin with the only other person worth talking to around here. Excuse me.'

Once she's gone, I flop back onto my bed, defeated. The only other person worth talking to around here, really? Harper and Phoenix aren't exactly close, I don't think.

My PA digs into my right shoulder. Rolling over, I grasp it and bring up the internet browser again. *Click here for your free Eternity trial. First 30 days free!*

I can't exactly play Eternity on my PA — it's way too small — but I'll be able to cast it to the screen in the common room. So why am I hesitating?

I'm not.

I tap on the icon. A pair of moons begin to rotate around each other on the screen, faster and faster, and then disappear, to be replaced by a rotating spiral.

Not just a rotating spiral. A whirlpool. Not just a whirlpool, but a—

'Define vortex,' I whisper.

FORTY-TWO

VIOLET

On Tuesday, Boxing Day, I wake to find that I am alone. Phoenix has left a note on the kitchen bench: *Gone for a wander, catch you later.*

Later? What's that supposed to mean? The world outside the window looks cold and white, fresh snow covering every surface. Checking my PA, I see it's half past eight already. Perhaps my sleep patterns have adjusted to Berlin time, although I was awake for a while around four am. I'd decided to check in with Ethan to let him know I hadn't forgotten about him.

It wasn't the best conversation we've ever had. Ethan was telling me how the game he and Rawiri had designed was making mega-bucks, how he reckoned the Foundation had stolen it and altered it somehow.

I mean, it was good, he'd said. *But not that good.*

Have you played it to see if it's different? I'd thought-asked, wondering if he was just being modest.

Not yet. Ethan had sounded frustrated. *We've been working out with Dash all morning. He's been teaching us how to fight people with knives.*

Ugh, I'd thought-said, although knives are the least of my worries. I'm more interested in learning how to intercept Holistic fanatics with access to the deadliest virus known to humans.

Also, I was trying to block off the parts of my memory that I didn't want Ethan to see. Not that there was anything for him to see, because nothing had happened with Phoenix, nothing at all.

Almost nothing.

I must have zoned out, because Ethan had thought-said, *Violet? Are you there?*

Yeah, sorry, I'm a bit . . . sleepy. Will you get a chance to play your game later?

Maybe tonight. We're going skydiving this afternoon.

Skydiving?

Uh-huh. Ethan had brightened. *We're going up in a plane. Obviously.*

That sounds really cool.

It does. He'd hesitated. *Are you OK?*

Apart from being across the other side of the world from you, yeah, of course. Why?

Because you sound kind of . . . I don't know, distracted. He didn't add, *There's something you're not telling me.* He didn't have to. He wasn't blocking me.

And yet . . . yet, I was semi-blocking him, and he knew it.

I am distracted, I'd thought-said. *I can't help thinking about everything we have to do.*

Are you scared?

Kind of. But we'll be OK. All we have to do is find enough evidence for the ITA to arrest the suspects. It's not as if we're going to be fighting them or anything. Except . . . I'd wondered if I should block my next thought, my budding idea. I didn't.

NO, VIOLET. His words were solid, black, shouty capitals. *NO, YOU CAN'T. YOU COULD DIE. NOT JUST YOU, BUT HUNDREDS OF OTHERS TOO.*

But I have to take the chance. This could be the only way to get one up on the Foundation so they give us our freedom. If I don't, we'll never get to be together. They'll make sure of it.

I think you should forget about it. Just do what you have to do and come back. Then his thought-stream had begun to scatter, and he'd thought-said, *Hey, Vi, I've got to get ready for the skydive. Be careful, OK?*

I'll be careful. I'd turned, pressed my nose into my pillow. Just do what you have to do? 'This *is* what I have to do,' I'd whispered.

And now it's five pm in Darwin, and I could talk to Ethan again, could ask him how his skydive went. I could, but part of me knows it's better if I don't. I need to focus.

I hear a door open, feel a rush of fridge-cool air. 'Hey,' Phoenix says.

'Hey.' I turn. Phoenix is holding a baguette, the tip of his nose frosty-pink. 'How was your walk?' I ask. So formal, as if we're an elderly couple. We've only communicated with spoken words since our tussle in the Tiergarten yesterday, when I'd picked up on the emotions Phoenix usually tried so hard to hide.

(When I kissed her . . .)

'Cold.' Phoenix dumped the bread on the bench. 'I decided to go back past Thomas and Klara's apartment.'

(she tasted like maple syrup and I . . .)

'Were they home?' I push the memory away, the one that chased me into my dreams, where I was reminded that Phoenix had tasted like coffee and honey, the one that reminded me how his stubble had felt against my cheek.

(wish we . . .)

Phoenix's voice weaves through the clamour in my brain. 'Yeah. I accessed Klara. I don't know why we have to be so much closer to non-VORTEX people to access them.'

I shrug. 'I don't know, I guess because it's a two-way thing with us. What were they doing?'

'Having breakfast.' He perches on a stool. 'Klara was struggling to feed Mia, something to do with a feeding tube. But she was also thinking about going in to work tonight.'

'At the research facility?'

'At Präzision, yeah. She was nervous because she wasn't sure she was going to be able to get into the areas with high-level biosecurity clearance. She and Thomas kind of had this argument about it.'

'Really? What did they say?'

Phoenix breaks off a piece of bread. 'She said, "Isn't it enough to get rid of the whole problem?" And he said it was too dangerous, that they could end up dispersing *it* all over Berlin.'

'By *it*, he means Javier virus.' My heart speeds up. 'So he wants Klara to get the Javier broth out before they blow the place up?'

'I think so. But when I fixed on Thomas, all I got was him fretting about this meeting with Dieter today. I reckon Dieter's got something to do with whatever they're going to use to destroy the research facility. It'll be easier if we're somewhere close when Thomas and Dieter meet up.'

I know he's right. Even though we got a fix on Thomas and Klara, it's not that easy to tune into them for more than a few minutes. The further we got away from them, the patchier their thought-streams became, like a bad PA signal. Phoenix is right; communication is so much easier between VORTEX members.

'OK, if you know where they're meeting, then sure.'

'Yes, Thomas was working out what time he'd have to leave to get there, so I have a good idea.'

Trying to hide my mounting anxiety, I start flicking through news items on my PA. 'Oh. Hey.' When Phoenix quirks an eyebrow at me, I read the headline aloud: *Eternity creators die but game lives on: best VirtReal sim ever, say teens from around the globe.*

Phoenix peers over my shoulder. 'Whoa, Ethan made this?'

'Ethan and his friend Rawiri, yeah. But Ethan says it's been altered, potentially by the Foundation.'

'Why would they want to do that?'

'To make money?' I reach for the bread. 'Or maybe they're trying to suck people in, indoctrinate them or something.'

'Hmm.' Phoenix stands up and strolls into the kitchen. 'Coffee?'

'Sure,' I say.

There's not much else to do until Thomas meets Dieter at lunch time, so Phoenix and I turn into tourists again. After a breakfast of coffee and chocolate spread on French bread, we set off for Checkpoint Charlie. I've always been fascinated by the wall which used to divide East and West Berlin, and the checkpoint that was heavily guarded until the wall fell.

I don't know what I expected to see. Chunks of wall, maybe, or some sort of secret tunnel.

'Guess it was more impressive when the wall was actually here.' Phoenix strolls around the miniature replica hut. 'Want to take a selfie?'

'No, are you crazy?'

He catches my eye for a moment and I sense it again, the new thing that has sprung up since I don't know when. He's blocking me. I'm blocking him too.

'Some would say so,' he says after a few seconds.

'Only foreigners used to be able to cross through here,' I say, taking a photo anyway, but not with me in it. Phoenix blinks, as if surprised that I would want to capture his image. I think of a saying I once heard — *take only photos, leave only footprints* — and wonder if that applies to us. No one said we shouldn't leave part of ourselves here. So when Phoenix goes to take my photo next, I let him.

At ten to twelve, I sit opposite Phoenix at a pub near Alexanderplatz, contemplating the gigantic slab of meat on my plate.

'This Wiener schnitzel is bigger than me,' I say.

Phoenix grins, taps the side of his beer glass. 'And this is nearly bigger than me.' He's sipping from a stein, which, according to him, holds two pints of beer.

'Are you really going to drink all of that?'

'You can help me,' he murmurs, leaning back to let the waiter deposit a plate in front of him with an equally gigantic pork knuckle and sauerkraut.

'I don't drink beer,' I say, but I take a sip anyway before taking off my scarf and jersey. We're sitting by the fire, light and shadows dancing over our table. It feels more like late evening than the middle of the day.

That's because, Phoenix begins.

Jet lag, I know. I frown, listening as a familiar thought-stream grows louder. *Can you hear that?*

Phoenix goes very still. Thomas' thought-stream is very clear, and there's a new one, too.

Dieter, Phoenix think-says. I nod, dig my fork into my schnitzel. From what I can hear, it's clear that Dieter doesn't trust Thomas, and Thomas doesn't trust Dieter either. So why are they having lunch together?

Listen, Phoenix think-says, so I do. Dieter and Thomas are discussing Thomas' research, something to do with 'transfer of data'.

Data, Phoenix think-says. *Yeah, right.*

Ssh, I think-say, and he falls silent again. Half an hour later, we've barely touched our food but the empty stein sits between us. I don't feel hungry anymore, not after what I've just heard.

Holy crap, Phoenix think-says, wiping foam off his upper lip. *That's all we need, isn't it?* Because now we have enough information for the ITA to arrest its suspects, or at the very least remove their weapons. The location of the data, or explosives, that Thomas plans to use in two days' time is very clear. Unless Dieter's thought-stream is a complete fabrication, the explosives are located in the wardrobe of his tiny apartment in the former East Berlin.

No, I think-reply. *It's not all we need.* My head is whirling, and it's got nothing to do with the half-stein of beer I just drank.

Jesus, Vi. Phoenix leans forward, clasps my wrist. *When did you dream that up? Are you crazy?*

Not at all. I slip my arm from his grasp and pick up my knife. *I'm determined.*

And dangerous as hell. There's a new respect in his tone, I think, although he's blocking me again, so it's hard to tell. Perhaps I should have blocked him, too, before he found out exactly what I'm planning, but I'm going to need his help.

Think of it as security, I think-say. *For later.*

FORTY-THREE:

ETHAN

t's early morning — so early the sun is still a smear on the horizon — and I am playing the game.

I'm not just playing the game. I *am* the game.

I've been in the common room since eleven pm last night, when everyone else went to sleep. Once I started playing, I couldn't stop.

At first it didn't seem too different from the last time I'd played. After selecting Roman, as always, I'd leapt onto my trusty steed and navigated through a familiar set of obstacles: circling hawks which I'd chased away with arrows, a pair of wild-eyed Meth Heads whom I'd defeated with hand-to-hand combat, a witch disguised as an evil woman carrying a basket of fruit.

People are addicted to this? I'd thought. Perhaps I was underestimating our game.

I'd been playing for a couple of hours when I reached the Valley of Needles, a valley containing thousands of mutant cacti with poisoned spikes. Easy enough if you know the trick to navigating it, which is to obtain armour for my horse and myself before we enter. We'd purchased the armour from a dwarf in a nearby village, in exchange for the basket of fruit I'd taken from the slain witch. We were halfway through the cacti when I saw blurred figures in the distance.

'Huh?' I'd adjusted my VirtReal glasses, which I'd managed to pilfer from the VirtSim room earlier. As they drew closer, I saw the figures were young men with olive skin and teal-coloured irises.

'Greetings.' The dark-haired one raised his staff and I noticed a tattoo on the left bicep.

Not just any tattoo. A spiral tattoo.

'What the hell?' I'd whispered, and my heart had skipped a beat, which was something it hadn't done in ages. Too distracted to pay much attention to that, I noticed the shorter, blonder guy also had a spiral tattoo on his left bicep. On their right biceps, each had a Rod of Asclepius tattoo.

Just like Rawiri and me, I'd thought, rubbing my own tattooed biceps.

'Greetings,' I'd said into my microphone, while noting that the dark-haired guy was holding his staff in his left hand. My heart had skipped another beat. Rawiri's characters were always left-handed, just like him.

But he's dead . . . isn't he?

And so am I, apparently, I thought, and stifled a sudden inexplicable urge to laugh.

'I am Bill,' the dark-haired guy had said.

'And I am Gill,' the blond guy had said.

'I am Roman,' I'd responded, even as the names of the new characters echoed around my brain. *Bill and Gill*. Almost, but not quite, the nicknames my sister and I used for each other.

Bill and Gill.

Bill and Jill.

Were the names an accident?

My heart had skittered again. No, no, there were just too many coincidences.

Are you trying to communicate with me, Rawiri? I'd thought. But of course, there was no answer.

More horses began to weave between the cacti, their metallic-plated legs flashing beneath the twin suns. On each horse sat an olive-skinned teenager with teal eyes and identical tattoos.

'We are the children who survived the Plague,' they'd intoned. 'And you, my friend, are fucked.'

Rawiri. How many times had I told him not to drop the f-bomb in our game?

'Rawiri,' I'd whispered. 'Where are you?'

There was no answer. But I had clues, enough clues to make me think — hope — that Rawiri might be alive after all.

Perhaps, if I kept going, there'd be more.

It's seven hours later, and I'm still going. My eyes feel like boiled onions, my throat as though I've swallowed a cup of desert sand. I should have a break, rehydrate, get some sleep. But I can't, because I've nearly finished the game. I can't, because every now and then words appear on the screen, urging me on. The game is *next level* all right. It's gone far beyond anything Rawiri and I ever devised.

You have reached level 21. Only ten other players have reached this level to date.

You have reached level 27. Only two other players have reached this level to date.

And finally, half an hour ago: *You have reached the thirtieth and final level. Only one other player has reached, and failed to pass, this level. May the luck of the gods be with you.*

And now I am dangling headfirst over a bubbling pit of acid while the Grand Magus flings riddles at me, faster and faster. I have two minutes to solve each riddle. If I go over two minutes, the Magus's Hunchbacked Gaoler will swing his sword through the rope holding me above the pit and I'll fall to my death.

But I am keeping up. I am, I am.

I'm struggling to solve the last riddle, one where I'm trying to determine the identities of three Roman gods, whose names are True, False and Random, with yes-no questions. The gods can only answer in their own language, and each god speaks a different language. It's almost too much to wrap even my virally optimised brain around.

I fling the last of my answers at the Grand Magus. *God B is True. God C is False. God A is Random.*

'Too clever,' the Grand Magus mocks. 'Too clever, too clever.'

Spirals begin to whirl in front of my eyes, faster and faster, until all I can see is stars. Stars and a pair of pendant-like moons hanging in the sky. The Grand Magus is gone, and so is the Citadel of Cirrus.

'Congratulations,' a voice says. 'You are the Legend of Asclepius. The Spiral Kingdom is yours.'

I take the headphones and VirtReal glasses off. Rub my eyes. Reach for my water bottle.

How the hell do you expect anyone else to solve this? I ask the ever-silent Rawiri. *There's no way anyone else could do all of those riddles in two minutes each, let alone design this, not unless they've been . . .*

Exactly, a voice whispers in my brain. Maybe the voice is a figment of my imagination, and maybe it isn't, but I know this:

Eternity has been virally optimised, and I am the first person to solve it.

I stand up, swaying slightly. I have work to do, more riddles to solve. But first, I need to talk to Violet, and then I need to sleep.

It's six am.

FORTY-FOUR:

VIOLET

t's nine-thirty pm, three and a half hours since Klara started her evening shift at Präzision. At midnight, she will go home, hopefully with the Javier broth in her possession. We will have to wait until the next morning, once Thomas has gone to work and Klara has left to take Mia to the physiotherapist, and the apartment is empty.

Phoenix is stretched out on the couch, already asleep. I wish I could do the same, but my body clock is topsy-turvy, upside down and inside out.

I'm sitting on the bed, trying to concentrate on an e-book on my PA, when I feel a twinge, followed by a thought-shimmer.

Hey, I think-say, a yellow burst of happiness igniting inside me. *You're up early.*

Or up late, depending on which way you want to look at it. Ethan's fatigue is washed-denim, his thought-stream slower than usual.

Really? What have you been doing? Recalling our last conversation, I think-say, *Wait, have you been playing the game all night?*

Yeah. I just finished.

And was it different, like you thought?

I picture him rubbing his eyes, lying back on his bed. *Yes and no*, he replies. *The essence of it was the same, but there were all these new challenges, and new characters that only Rawiri could have created.*

So the Foundation have nothing to do with it, then?

I'm not so sure about that. Like all the players are saying, it's next level. There's no way the old Rawiri could have created that. There's no way the old Ethan could have solved it either.

Even though you created it?

No, that's what I'm trying to tell you. It's way beyond what we ever dreamed of. I think Rawiri finished it, but only once he'd been . . . altered. Like us.

Altered how? By getting sick?

Or by someone making him sick, Ethan think-says, and now I'm seeing rows of teenagers in pods again, the dream that Ethan thinks is definitely not a dream. If he's right, the Foundation staff are inoculating teenagers with M-fever to make more of us.

I twist the edge of my blanket between my fingers. *But why would the Foundation let this game be released?*

Because, Ethan think-says, *they're looking for others.*

Others? You mean . . . I sit bolt upright. *Others like us?*

Exactly. While I'm still trying to digest the implications of that, Ethan adds, *Vi, I'm so tired. I have to go to sleep now. But promise me you won't do anything stupid.*

I won't do anything stupid, I think-reply. *I promise. Talk to you later, OK?*

Later, yeah. I can already sense him slipping into sleep, his thought waves slower than ever.

I've never felt so awake in my life.

At nine am, which is five-thirty pm in Darwin, Phoenix and I stand in a stairwell, arguing in our usual way — in silence.

Phoenix gestures towards the door, behind which is Thomas and Klara's apartment. *I'm not going to let you go in there by yourself. Are you crazy?*

I cross my arms. *How is asking you to stand guard outside being crazy?*

I'll be able to hear someone if they're coming. He taps his temple. *Remember?*

Like I keep telling you, I flare, *I'm not as stupid as you think. And if someone does come, you'll be able to intercept them that much sooner.*

Fine, he snaps. *I'll stay out here. But load your gun.*

I don't need to—

Just do it, will you?

I load my gun and carefully place it in my jacket pocket, yank on the bottom of my bullet-proof vest. *Satisfied?*

I guess I'll have to be. Make it quick.

I'll try my best.

After leaving Mr Know-It-All in the stairwell, I hold my PA up to the retinal sensor outside Thomas and Klara's apartment. Within seconds, I hear the locks slide. I don't quite know how it works — something to do with resetting the encoded information in the retinal sensor — but whatever, the door is swinging open now.

The apartment is bigger than ours, but not much, with a Christmas tree laden with lights and baubles in the lounge. I move into the hallway, passing a bathroom and a bedroom decorated with stars and rainbows before heading to the main bedroom down the end.

Unless Klara has changed her mind since I last accessed her, the cylinder containing the deadly broth will be safely stowed in a suitcase beneath her bed.

Pausing in the doorway, I take in the photographs on the wall. The first photo is of a younger Thomas and Klara kissing beneath an oak tree on their wedding day. The second photo is of a chubby baby who must be only a few months old. The baby is lying naked on a sheepskin rug and laughing up at the camera, her eyes sparkling. Mia, before she got sick.

Have you found it? Phoenix sounds irritated, but beneath that, I can sense his nervousness.

Give me a chance, will you?

I drop to my knees and peer beneath the bed. No suitcase, what the hell? I stand up again and swivel, my eyes settling on the wardrobe. The doors are firmly closed, a freshly ironed linen shirt dangling from a clothes hanger. I yank on the knob and use the torch on my PA to peer inside.

'Bingo,' I whisper.

Found it?

I found the suitcase. Relax, will you?

After pulling out a large, metallic-blue suitcase, I crouch to unzip it. It's stuffed with jerseys, business shirts, a pair of leather trousers. I place items on the floor beside me until the suitcase is empty, completely empty. Great, just great.

Phoenix's voice intrudes again. *Haven't found it yet?*

My irritation growing — I wish he'd shut up for a few minutes so I can concentrate — I spring to my feet and peer into the wardrobe again, angling my torch upward this time. There's a shelf up there, with a smaller, cabin-baggage-sized suitcase sitting on it. *Yes.*

I tug the suitcase forwards, nearly hitting myself on the head when it falls towards me, and place it on the bed. There are clothes in this suitcase too, socks and tights mostly, but this time there's something beneath them, something hard. My heart gives out an extra-loud thud. This is it, got to be.

And if it's not, then it's time to leave, Phoenix think-says.

Shut up, will you?

I lift the item out. It's a cardboard box, not much bigger than those used to hold coffee mugs in stores. When I shine my torch inside, I see a metal canister, approximately the size and shape of a cigar. The yellow sticker on the outside has a symbol comprised of three interlocking rings and BIOHAZARD in capital letters beneath it. I figure the canister is temperature-controlled, because there's a digital display on the outside that reads 37C. When I peer inside, I glimpse a glass vial containing a turbid brown liquid.

A turbid brown liquid swimming with Javier virus.

And suddenly my heart is going crazy, and at first I think it's just me, until I realise it's Phoenix's panic I'm feeling, Phoenix's colour flooding through me and its red red red and he think-shouts, *Run Violet get out get out someone's in there I don't know how she's—*

And I turn, still gripping the vial

Right before I feel something hit me just below the kidneys and

At first I think I've been punched but then

It's cold and sharp and I can't

Breathe

And she says, 'Did you really think we wouldn't find out?' Right before I feel the knife slide into me again, sharp-sharp between my ribs oh God

And I hear two loud cracks and Phoenix is yelling with his

voice this time, 'No, no, no,' and I hear moaning and I don't
know if it's me or her
    And I spin and fall
    And fall
    And

FORTY-FIVE

ETHAN

t's late afternoon and I've been limping through the day, low on energy after two hours sleep. At five pm, Dash tells me I'm as good as useless after I hit my head when trying to do a flying forward roll.

'Go have a nap,' he says. 'Before you injure yourself or someone else.'

I wake drenched in sweat an indeterminate time later, my heart galloping. In my dreams, there was shouting.

Run Violet get out get out someone's in there

I sit up. But it was just a . . .

Oh God

My heart isn't slowing. I press my palm to my chest, squint at my PA. 5.43 pm.

Something is

Red red red

My breath quickening, I try to fix on Violet, but all I get is

Sharp sharp sharp

My heart, our heart, is hitting my ribs like a hammer

And Phoenix, I can hear him now, and he's saying

Oh God oh God Violet don't move
And it's not a dream it's not a dream it's not a dream

FORTY-SIX

VIOLET

The world inside is cold and grey grey grey. I can't move, can hardly breathe for the pain. Phoenix is calling out to me but I can't hear what he's saying and I'm slipping Into a place where it doesn't hurt quite so

Hang in there Violet do you remember asking me if you could heal yourself concentrate

And my heart can hardly keep up with

So much blood

FORTY-SEVEN:

ETHAN

i leap out of bed, my hand still on my chest, on our heart.

Phoenix, I think-shout. *Phoenix, can you hear me?* I'm terrified it won't work, that I won't reach him, but seconds later, his panicked thoughts swirl through mine.

Ethan oh God someone stabbed Violet she's bleeding.

For a time after that our communication is wordless, eddies of fear and anger and I-don't-know-what, until Phoenix's words break through again: *We're in the ambulance they're giving her blood but she's lost so much her blood pressure is rock bottom they're doing CPR oh God*.

And I can feel it, can feel how her heart, our heart, is struggling, and Phoenix says, *Ethan her heart can't keep up with both of you, she's lost so much blood*.

And I know what he says is true but I don't know how to disengage from her, I don't.

But if I don't, she'll die. I suck in an agonised breath, try to reach her through the

Red sharp red sharp

And I say, *Violet, I love you, please don't die*.

And I'm crying now, so scared, even as my dream-flow begins to swirl, faster and faster.

And I push, up and out, as hard as I can

And I'm flying high, above my body, above the Foundation, seeking the stars and the moon and the spiral galaxy that binds

And I feel the moment I disengage from her, a gut-wrenching pain, and the Milky Way floods into my eyes

And I can't feel my heart, our heart, anymore but now I know this:

Going back hurts like hell

And not going back

Doesn't hurt at all.

FORTY-EIGHT

VIOLET

The world is white and bright and terrifying. Every breath I take is a jagged glass in my chest, a ripping-tearing in my back. My heart beats an agonised rhythm.

An agonised, singular rhythm.

'Just breathe,' a voice says and I cough, a cough that turns into a strangled gasp. Someone is squeezing my hand. Someone is whispering in my ear.

Violet, you're OK, you're OK.

No, not in my ear.

I open my eyes, stare into a pair of dove-grey irises. Phoenix. Wolf Black. Black Wolf.

Johnno.

Phoenix flinches. 'You're going to be OK,' he says, glancing at someone out of my view. I turn my head and nearly stop breathing when I see who is sitting on the other side of me.

'Violet.' Melody strokes my brow. 'The worst is over.'

I open my mouth, close it again. There's a background noise I recognise but can't quite place at first, not until I see the curved ceiling above my head.

'Plane,' I croak, and Melody says, 'Yes, you're in a plane. We're taking you home.'

'New Zealand?'

As soon as the words are out of my mouth, I know how impossible that is. *Oh my God, oh my God, I'm going back to Australia?*

But then my heart lurches because I realise I will be seeing Ethan soon.

And yet, something is. Not. Quite. Right.

Violet, Phoenix says, and his colour is deep blue, so murky I can barely discern what lies beneath.

Melody's words come thick and fast, like the confused thoughts tumbling through my brain. 'Induced coma for the past week . . . collapsed lung . . . seventeen bags of blood . . . miracle you survived at all . . . never seen anyone heal so . . .'

I'm not listening. I'm not listening, because Phoenix is think-saying, *I'm sorry, Vi, I'm so sorry*, and when I look at him his irises are glistening.

What do you mean? It wasn't your fault. It's my fault, I think, for being so reckless.

He doesn't answer. There's something else, something he wants to tell me but can't.

Phoenix, I think-say, and then, as if it will help, *Johnno*.

He flinches again. *Vi, I—*

Melody says, 'Phoenix saved your life. You're lucky he acted so fast.'

'Who was it?' I say. 'Who stabbed me?'

'I don't know who she was. But I shot her. Twice, in the head.' Phoenix's voice is dull. 'She was in the apartment the whole time. I should have been more careful.'

'*We* should have been more careful.' Why is he being so hard on himself?

Phoenix takes a deep breath, looks at Melody. 'Are you going to tell her?'

Melody presses her lips together. 'Later. She needs to rest.'

'Tell me what?' When neither of them replies, I repeat, 'Tell me *what*?' even though every word is a knife blade between my ribs.

'Violet,' Melody says gently, 'Ethan had a cardiac arrest on the same night you were taken to hospital. We tried to resuscitate him, but by the time we found him—'

I can't breathe. I can't breathe, I can't breathe. Phoenix touches my arm. I shake him off, whimpering with pain.

'You promised you'd keep him safe.' My voice rises. 'I asked you to monitor him. You said you would, you *said*.'

Melody seems close to tears, too. 'We were monitoring his heart. We ran as soon as the alarms went off and did CPR for almost an hour, but it was no good.'

I'm sorry, Phoenix think-says again, and now I'm getting it all, the whole blast of memories, his and mine, patchy though mine are, and the voices are saying

Oh God

They're saying

Phoenix is saying

Ethan her heart can't keep up with both of you, she's lost so much blood.

Oh my God, I think-say. *Oh my God, you didn't?*

Phoenix stands up, his face ashen. *You were dying. If he hadn't released you, you'd both be dead. I'm sorry, I had to tell him, I had no other choice.*

And I'm remembering Ethan's last words filtering through to me, as I lay bleeding out in a bedroom in Berlin: *Violet, I love you, please don't die.*

'No!' I yell. 'No, no!' And I'm shaking and gasping and crying and Phoenix is trying to hold me and I hit out at him and scream with pain-fury-grief, and suddenly two men appear, flight crew, and they're holding my arms and Melody injects something into the plastic tubing running into my vein while I scream the same thing over and over and over.

I hate you, I hate you, I hate you.

And I fall and fall and fall.

FORTY-NINE:

VIOLET

In January, the heavens open, or maybe it's hell. It rains and rains. If I were less cynical, I'd think the world is crying for me, but I know that's not true.

I'm determined not to cry anymore either. It never solves anything, never helps anyone, least of all me.

At night time, the others go travelling, each widening the reach of their dream-flow. Audrey tells me how she flew over Alice Springs the other night. *Come with us*, she says. *It'll take your mind off things, help you relax.* But I don't want to forget. I don't want to relax.

Callum and Harper are preparing for their mission. On the thirty-first of January, they'll be flown to London to try and avert another terrorist attack. Audrey is happy to bide her time. As for Phoenix, I only speak to him once in the whole month of January, when he dares to knock on the door of my room.

It's almost a month since a faceless woman tried to cut me to ribbons and Ethan's heart stopped forever. I'm sitting in my room, holding a notebook. It was amongst the box of Ethan's possessions Melody gave me this morning. I don't know why she waited so long. Maybe she thought I wouldn't be able to handle touching his stuff. Maybe she's right.

The notebook has a black cover and unlined pages. Ethan has filled the first several pages with sketches, mostly of the Foundation buildings and surroundings. Some of the sketches are bird's-eye views of the massive rock formations and canyons we used to fly over every night, even as our earthly bodies lay trapped in our rooms.

Before.

Conditioning. Intensification. Bavaria. The prototype.

The prototype? Bavaria? What's that supposed to mean?

I flick forward to the last entry in the notebook, at what Ethan was writing before he set it aside for the last time.

Eternity. Asclepius. Spiral. Tattoos. Left-handed? Rawiri? Tracking.

Eternity. Ethan and Rawiri's game. The game Ethan thought Rawiri had taken to the *next level*. The game Ethan was convinced the Foundation were using to find others like us.

I re-read the notes. *Asclepius. Spiral. Tattoos.*

Remembering Ethan's Rod of Asclepius tattoo, my vision blurs. I never got to see him after he died, have no idea what they did with his body.

I wouldn't visit his grave even if I knew where it was. What good would it do? He wouldn't be there. I don't believe in life after death, don't believe in spirits.

There is a rap on my door, and I jump, look up to see *him* standing in the doorway.

Wolf Black. Black Wolf.

(When I kissed her . . .)

'Go away,' I say reflexively.

(she tasted like maple syrup and I . . .)

Phoenix stays where he is, clenching and unclenching his fists. *I need to give you something*, he think-says.

(wish we . . .)

I don't want it. I consider throwing something at him, but the only thing within reach is Ethan's PA.

I think you do. He steps inside, closing the door behind him. I could spit at him. I would, but he's taking something out of his trousers pocket, something that makes my stomach curl into a ball.

How long have you had that?

Since Berlin. Phoenix places the bubble-wrapped package on the foot of my bed, then backs away. *I hid it before the ambulance came. I knew how important it was to you.*

Pity you didn't consider that when you told Ethan to 'let me go'. I pick up the package and stare through the plastic at the metal cylinder. Inside that, I know, is a glass vial labelled with a Biohazard sticker.

I smuggled it inside a beanie in my suitcase all the way from Berlin, he think-says. *I could have turned it in to the authorities, or the Foundation staff. Don't think I haven't thought about it*. When I don't reply, he takes a deep breath. *I've got something else to tell you too, something important.*

I don't want to listen to him, but he's in my head already, his words slicing through me like glass. *The woman who stabbed you*, he think-says, *I never heard her, never got her thought-stream. After I shot her, I saw why*. He touches his ear.

A blocking device? I'm trying not to see the rest of the image in Phoenix's memory, trying not to see the bloody remains of the woman's head. *Where the hell did she get that? And who was she?*

Phoenix shakes his head, slowly, slowly, but I can hear what he's thinking loud and clear. *Either the woman stole it or someone betrayed us. Someone from the Foundation.*

I stare at the box. Think of the terrorists. Think of the knife sliding between my ribs. Think of Melody and Bruno and Marlow and everyone else I hate, including Phoenix.

Including Phoenix.

I look up, fix my gaze on his. 'I will never forgive you,' I say. 'Never, never. Do you hear me?'

Phoenix's jaw is clenched, his fists too. 'I hear you.'

Just as quickly, he's gone, the door clicking behind him. I grip the deadly package, counting heartbeats until the urge to cry passes.

You haven't died for nothing, Ethan, I vow. *And I will never forget you, never never.*

After wrapping the package in a t-shirt and stowing it my underwear drawer — I'll find a better hiding place for it soon — I stand by the window, gazing over the blood-red desert and stroking the implant buried beneath my skin.

I need to find out what the Foundation's true mission is. I need to work out if they are creating others like us, and why. I need to work out why the other VORTEX members seem so happy to accept their fate. Most of all, I need to ensure that the world finds out what has happened to Ethan, and why.

I won't forget you, Ethan, and the world won't either.

I promise you.

Welcome back, Violet Black.

ACKNOWLEDGEMENTS

A huge thank you to my friend and critique partner Nod, who, when I told her I was going to give up on writing this book 30,000 words in, said: 'I would have devoured a book like that when I was a kid.' I haven't looked back since and, eight months later, completed the third and final volume in the Black Spiral Trilogy. Thank you for your patient critique, Nod, and for all the times you told me something didn't make sense or was scientifically unbelievable! Thanks also to my son Lachie, who convinced me that I needed to write a trilogy rather than a two-book series; and to my friend and fellow author Rose Carlyle, who told me a few facts about the structure of a trilogy over lunch, thus inspiring me to finish book two (*Black Wolf*) nine weeks after writing the first sentence! Thank you to my husband Grant, for our spa conversations about futuristic fusion-powered vehicles, and to my daughter Maisie, who is always cracking the whip by asking 'what page are you up to?' and 'when do I get a copy of my own?'

I would like to acknowledge the use of the following quotes:

- 'Whoever fights monsters should see to it in the process that he does not become a monster. And if you gaze long enough into an abyss, the abyss will gaze back into you' on page 168 is attributed to Friedrich Nietzsche.
- 'Even the darkest night will end and the sun will rise' on

page 169 is from *Les Misérables*, by Victor Hugo.

^ 'And I asked myself about the present: how wide it was, how deep it was, how much was mine to keep' on page 172 is from *Slaughterhouse-Five*, by Kurt Vonnegut.

A big thank you to my fiction publisher Harriet Allan, for signing up this trilogy during one of the most difficult periods for publishing in history — a pandemic and Level 4 lockdown in New Zealand. I'm so grateful for your constant receptiveness, encouragement and wisdom, especially at this unpredictable time.

Thanks once again to Stu Lipshaw (managing editor), Cat Taylor (designer) and the rest of the amazing team at Penguin Random House for helping bring the first novel in the trilogy to fruition. I'd also like to thank my agent Nadine Rubin-Nathan, and the rest of the team at High Spot Literary, for their encouragement and helpful suggestions. Finally, thank you to the booksellers and librarians who help promote my work, and ultimately, *you*, the reader, without whom none of this would be possible.

BOOK 2 IN THE BLACK SPIRAL TRILOGY

BLACK WOLF

EILEEN MERRIMAN

NEXT IN THE BLACK SPIRAL TRILOGY

BLACK WOLF

ONE:

———

PHOENIX

i am running through the desert, the red earth firm and un-yielding beneath my trainers. It's twenty degrees Celsius, even at midnight. My chest is bare, my singlet knotted around my forehead to stop the sweat running into my eyes.

I could have chosen to leave my earthly body behind, to join the others in their nightly ritual soaring high above the desert, but I haven't done that since we returned from Berlin two months ago. I'm scared that if I leave my body behind, I won't want to return.

So I'm running, relishing the pain in my muscles, the burning in my lungs. For an hour I will forget who I am, what I have done. For an hour, I will be Phoenix again.

But in the morning, I know, I will wake with the heavy knowledge that I am the Black Wolf, never to be trusted, never to be loved — because the only people I've ever loved are either dead or hate my guts.

Violet won't even look at me. At breakfast, she sits at the opposite end of the table. During our physical training sessions, she takes care to avoid me, except in martial arts, where we swap partners every few minutes and she has no choice.

That's almost worse, having to touch someone who has the power to burn me with her thoughts alone.

At least, she would if I were allowed access to her thought-stream, but there's a permanent blockade coming from *that* direction.

That's fine, because I'm blocking her too.

This morning, Dash is taking me and the rest of the VORTEX members (aka Virally Optimised Telepaths, aka captives) through drills where we practise turning in for throws but don't actually throw each other. He's got us counting in different languages as we do it. First, Audrey counts in Japanese: *ichi, ni, san, shi.* Next, Callum counts in Māori: *tahi, rua, toru, whā.* Harper counts in Mandarin, and Violet in Russian.

It's my turn, and all I can think is: *eins, zwei, drei, vier.* But I can't count in German, not in front of Violet.

Harper says Violet must have post-traumatic stress disorder, following what happened in Berlin. Who wouldn't, after being stabbed twice in the back and nearly bleeding to death, after collapsing a lung and finding out her boyfriend had died while she was unconscious?

I say, 'Yeah, I guess she must.' And when I have occasional selfish thoughts like *No one asks about whether I get flashbacks too, because shooting a woman in the head and watching her die wasn't a bloody walk in the park, even if she was a terrorist,* I keep them to myself.

'Fletcher,' Dash barks, 'where's your brain?'

I want to tell him I left it in Berlin, but instead I start counting in French — *un, deux, trois, quatre* — as Violet twists and pulls me up on her shoulder again and again. When I get to *dix,* ten, she

bends her knees and sends me flying over her shoulder and —
wham — I'm blinking up at the ceiling, all the breath knocked
out of my lungs.

'Nice,' Dash says.

Violet doesn't say anything, just leaves me there and moves on
to her next partner, Callum.

No one says 'Man, burnt'. No one even thinks it. If they did,
I'd be sure to hear them.

No one dares, because it's no laughing matter that Violet hates
me because I killed her boyfriend, Ethan.

If I were her, I'd hate me too.

BOOK 3 IN THE BLACK SPIRAL TRILOGY

BLACK SPIRAL

EILEEN MERRIMAN

Wise, tough, heart-breaking, funny, this compulsive love story is about facing your demons.

Fifteen-year-old Rebecca McQuilten moves with her parents to a new city. Lonely but trying to fit in, she goes to a party, but that's when things really fall apart.

I couldn't tell anyone what had happened. Especially since I was the new girl in town. Who would want to believe me?

Things look up when she meets gregarious sixteen-year-old Cory Marshall.

'You're funny, Becs,' Cory said.
'You have no idea,' I said, and clearly he didn't, but I was smiling anyway. And after that, he was all I could think about.

Cory helps Rebecca believe in herself and piece her life back together; but that's before he shatters it all over again . . .

A moving novel about learning to find happiness in the face of uncertainty and discovering a love that transcends the boundary between life and death.

Seventeen-year-old Alex Byrd is about to have the worst day of her life, and the best. A routine blood test that will reveal her leukaemia has returned, but she also meets Jamie Orange.

Some people believe in love at first sight, and some don't.
I believe in love in four days.
I believe in falling.

Both teenagers have big dreams, but also big obstacles to overcome.

'Promise me you won't try to die,' I said. 'Ever.'
'Promise me you won't either,' he countered.
'It's not really something I can control.'

A moving story about unconventional love, bullying and being true to yourself.

'I wish I wasn't the weirdest sixteen-year-old guy in the universe.'

Felix would love to have been a number. Numbers have superpowers and they're safe — any problem they might throw up can be solved.

'If I were a five, I'd be shaped like a pentagon . . . there'd be magic in my walls, safety in my angles.'

People are so much harder to cope with. At least that's how it seems until Bailey Hunter arrives at school. Bailey has a stutter, but he can make friends and he's good at judo. And Bailey seems to have noticed Felix:

'Felix keeps to himself mostly, but there's something about him that keeps drawing me in.'

A missing girl, a secret diary and unsettling revelations . . .

Today is the first of September, the first day of spring, and it's been sixty-four days since I last saw Sophie Abercrombie. It's been sixty-four days since anyone saw Sophie Abercrombie.

The prettiest Sophie.
The missing Sophie.

As Sophie MacKenzie — Mac — confides to her diary, she last saw Sophie Abercrombie kissing James Bacon, their English teacher. Mac has passed this on to the police, but there is plenty she knows about James Bacon that she has kept to herself. She hasn't even told Twiggy, the third Sophie in their once tightknit threesome.

The Trio of Sophies is no more.

PRAISE FOR EILEEN MERRIMAN

Pieces of You

'the kind of book you want to read in one sitting because it is so breathtakingly good . . . It feels utterly real. It does not smudge the tough stuff. It is kaleidoscopic in both emotion and everyday detail . . . Eileen writes with such a flair for dialogue, for family circumstances, for teenage struggles and joys. This is the kind of book that will stay at the front of my mind all week and longer — I recommend it highly.' — Paula Green, *Poetry Shelf*

'. . . could well become one of the biggest local YA books of the year. It's intelligent, literate . . . pertinent, witty when it needs to be, thought-provoking and relatable.' — Dionne Christian, *NZ Herald*

'Merriman's acute observation and awareness of teen mentality comes to the fore. It all feels very real and fresh.'
— Denis Wright, *The Sapling*

Catch Me When You Fall

'My best pick for 2018 for young adults, the standout for me . . . it's kind of heart-wrenching and really real and quirky and a great teen read for girls and boys.' — James Russell, *Radio NZ*

This book . . . is interested in life and death struggles, and the way that these struggles interact with the more everyday agonies and ecstasies of coming-of-age . . . The story is well-paced and absorbing . . . effective in its depiction of the desperation inspired by love and fear of loss. — Angelina Sbroma, *NZ Books*

'When it comes to the medical details, the story pays impressive attention . . . the story doesn't only focus on Alex and her physical sickness but also on Jamie and his far subtler mental illness . . . well written and cleverly expressed.' — Madeleine Fountain, *NZ Doctor*

Invisibly Breathing

'. . . more than just a book to be read, but gripping literature which both celebrates love and also exposes society's harmful behaviour towards love that is not considered "conventional".
Rating 5/5 stars' — Faga Tuigamala, *Tearaway*

'dialogue is crisp and convincing and their characters are well drawn . . . a gripping account of two young men on the brink of manhood, uncertain and deeply involved emotionally, facing the reactions of their family and friends . . . It is a moving story, well told.'
— Trevor Agnew, *Magpies*

'It's a clever book. Ingenious chapter headings, smart sentences, inventive glides of plot and relationships. It's very contemporary, veined with phones and txts and Twitter and *Grand Theft Auto V*. There's a stadium-sized cast of kids, and Merriman gets their blitheness, erratic fuses, invulnerability-cum-fragility spot-on . . . her book is bloody good.' — David Hill, *NZ Books*

A Trio of Sophies

'I absolutely endorse this in a Young Adult Section, or High School Library. It could just save a life — and no I'm not being dramatic. It was a book that fifteen-year-old me needed to read, and that twenty-seven-year-old me is glad to have . . . Absolutely worth the five stars. And the late bedtime.' — Krystal B, *Goodreads*

'Fast-paced and unpredictable, *A Trio of Sophies* will keep readers on their toes and caught up until the last page. And if it's your first Merriman book, it certainly won't be your last.'
— Sarah Pollok, *Weekend Herald*

'This is a page turner make no bones about that . . . Much to enjoy in this novel. Best New Zealand YA novel of the year so far. Don't miss it, you will kick yourself if you do. The ending will make you think.' — Bob Docherty, *Bobsbooksnz.wordpress.com*

For more information about our titles
visit www.penguin.co.nz